Love Songs for the Quarantined

Also by K.L. Cook

Last Call
The Girl from Charnelle

Love Songs for the Quarantined

K.L. Cook

For Valerie & Bob —
Well met in Fairhope! These
songs's for you.

Cheers
Kenny

April 17, 2018

Willow Springs Editions
Spokane

Copyright © 2011 by K.L. Cook
All rights reserved.

This is a work of fiction. Names, characters, places, and incidents are either the product of the author's imagination or are used fictitiously.

ISBN: 978-0-9832317-0-7

Cover Art: Stephen Schultz, *Orpheus and Eurydice*, 1992, acryllic on canvas, 90" by 120"
Cover Design: Aimee Cervenka and Ann Huston
Author Photo: Deborah Ford

Printed in the United States of America.

These stories were published, sometimes in different form, in the following magazines, journals, and anthologies: "Bonnie and Clyde in the Backyard" and "The Man Who Fell from the Sky" in *Glimmer Train Stories*; "Orchestration" in *Harvard Review*; "The Couple Upstairs," "Chalkdust on a Dress," and "First Birth" in *Arts & Letters*; "Snipe Hunt" (as "Tableau") in *Alligator Juniper*; "When Our Son Died of Leukemia" in *South Dakota Review*; "Blind" in *Brevity*; "Wedding Photograph, June 1963" in *Wrong Tree Review*; "Bad Weather" in *94 Creations*; "A Nova, a Secret, an Eyelash, a Snoring Man" (as "A Nova, an Eyelash, a Snoring Man: Notes on Adolescent Summers") in *When I Was a Loser* (Free Press/Simon & Schuster); "Love Song for the Quarantined" in *The Louisville Review*; "Filament" in *One Story*; and "Relative Peace" in *Prairie Schooner*. "Bonnie and Clyde in the Backyard" was reprinted in *The Best of the West 2011: Stories from the Wide Side of the Missouri* (University of Texas Press) and won the 2011 Spur Award for Best Short Story from the Western Writers of America.

*For Carson, Tristan, Vivian, Lena
and Charissa*

Contents

I
Bonnie and Clyde in the Backyard • 13
The Man Who Fell From the Sky • 37

II
Wedding Photograph, June 1963 • 57
Blind • 59
Chalkdust on a Dress • 61
Bad Weather • 63
Snipe Hunt • 67
A Nova, a Secret, an Eyelash, a Snoring Man • 79

III
The Couple Upstairs • 91
First Birth • 95
When Our Son Died of Leukemia • 99
What They Didn't Tell You About the Vasectomy • 101
Love Song for the Quarantined • 119
Orchestration • 129

IV
Filament • 135
Relative Peace • 149

Acknowledgments • 171

Let us go then, you and I,

When the evening is spread out against the sky,

Like a patient etherized upon a table...

—T. S. Eliot, "The Love Song of J. Alfred Prufrock"

I

Bonnie and Clyde in the Backyard

My mother, Whit, and Clara are at church, so I put the Chopin that Doc Melbourne lent us on the Victrola to soothe my father into sleep. Whit and I slaughtered a hog early in the morning, and the meat will rot in the May sun if I don't tend to it. I sheathe the hog, dispose of the trimmings, and am hypnotically rinsing the blood from the slaughter slab when I see a car barrel down the road to our farmhouse. A plume of dirt billows behind. Who in the world would drive the farm road that fast? I clean my hands and run to the house as a beautiful sand-colored sedan brakes in front. It looks new, despite the dried mud blasted against the fenders and sideboards. The dust rises up and over the hood like a shroud. I squint and cover my face with my sleeve. Though I've never seen them in person, I know before they speak a word who they are. I scan the backseat for more passengers, but it's just the two of them.

"Your father named Zachary?" Clyde asks. Boyish, with a dark brown curl of greasy hair flopping on his forehead below his fedora, his voice is higher pitched than I imagined it would be. I wonder for a moment if I'm mistaken. Maybe they're just joyriding kids.

"Yep," I say.

"What's your name?"

"Riley."

"Glad to meet you. I'm your cousin, thrice removed. Clyde." I shake his small, calloused hand. "This here's my wife, Bonnie."

"I see handsome runs in the family," she says, and Clyde smiles.

I know they aren't married. I know everything about them. I know she was married once when she was sixteen to a thief named Roy Thornton. I know she was a waitress at Marco's Café in Dallas. I know Clyde has killed at least ten men by now, including four police officers. I know that Buck is dead, his face and skull practically shot clean off in an ambush in Platte City. I know about the banks in Oklahoma and Missouri and Louisiana and New Mexico. I know about Bonnie's aunt in Carlsbad and the policeman they kidnapped there and dropped off in San Antonio, the one that made them famous. And I know, as everyone else in the country knows at this point in 1934, that it's just a matter of time before they will be caught or killed.

"My father's been sick," I say.

"I'm sorry to hear that," Clyde says. "What's wrong?"

"Something's the matter with his head."

He laughs. "You can say that about most the folks in Texas."

Bonnie slaps his arm. "Be respectful," she says. And then to me, "Don't mind him none. He's just like that. How's your daddy doing?"

"Not too well."

"Can we see him?" Clyde asks, suddenly serious. "He was nice to me when I was a boy. My mom's favorite cousin. She made me promise to stop by and pass on her good wishes."

I nod.

"Good deal," he says.

They step out of the car. The sight of them surprises me. So little. From the stories about them in the papers, I expect size, a certain grandeur. Yet she isn't even five feet tall, a girlish wisp, though prettier in person than in the newspaper photos, her skin pale, almost translucent, with freckles and a big, pretty smile and almost straight teeth. Her reddish-blonde hair twirls in ringlets to the bottom of her neck. A bright red skirt and a matching sweater cling to her body. I glimpse, at the skirt's hem, white gauze wrapped around her leg.

Clyde isn't much bigger, certainly no bigger than I am at thirteen. The coroner's report will later say that he was five-seven and weighed a hundred and thirty pounds. When he takes off his hat, his thick brown hair makes his head look too large for his body, as if he is a little girl's doll. He has an oval-shaped face with baby fat and freckles, a kid's face, complete with a couple of nicks on his cheeks and a scab on his forehead. He sports a green-and-red-striped tie, like a Christmas dandy, but his shirt is spattered with either dirt or blood. He walks with a slight limp, a pistol tucked into the front of his pants. My mother won't appreciate that pistol. She won't appreciate this visit at all. But I am not about to tell Clyde Barrow, cousin or not, that he can't carry a gun onto our property.

"The rest of your family here?" Clyde asks.

"They went to church."

He nods.

"Clyde, the car," Bonnie says.

"You got a barn, son?" Clyde asks. I point to the north side of the house, beyond the stand of peach trees. "You think your father'd mind if I parked my car in there?"

"I guess not."

"Why don't you give the boy a ride?" Bonnie says.

"I'll do one better." Clyde tosses me the keys. "You know how to drive, don't you?"

"Yes, sir."

"Well then."

I get in the car, and Bonnie climbs in with me. Her skirt rises. The bandage extends beyond her knee to her thigh.

She catches me looking. "An accident," she says. "But I'm better now. Clyde nursed me back to health, the sugar."

I turn the key, and the engine starts right up, without any trouble, just hums.

"This is nice, ain't it?"

"Yes, ma'am."

"Feel these custom seats." She places her little hand on mine and runs my fingers over the upholstery. "It's also got a built-in water-style heater." She turns it on, and hot air pours like the breath of a horse from the vents. "Not that we need it in this weather, huh?"

Clyde pokes his head inside my window. He smells, strangely, like sweat and oranges. "She sure is sweet on this damn car," he says. "Let's put her away."

I inch the sedan along. At the barn, Clyde says he'll get the doors. He limps over and swings them open. The chickens squawk and flutter, sounding an alarm, but he walks in like it's his place, not ours, and I roll the car over the hay-strewn ground until he holds up his hand for me to stop. Bonnie and I get out, and I drop the keys in Clyde's small hand.

"Thanks," I say.

"The pleasure's mine, son." It sounds odd, him calling me *son*, since he doesn't seem much older than me, though of course I know that what he's done over the past few years—including the stint in Eastham prison—is enough for any lifetime.

Bonnie and I stand on either side of him while he opens the trunk. About a dozen guns clutter the padded floor, including revolvers, rifles, and two of the automatics called BARs that I've seen in the newspapers and magazines. There's a crate of oranges there and a box of license plates. Clyde smiles at me, proud of his stash. I try not to reveal any surprise, but my face must please him because he and Bonnie both laugh.

"What'll it be?" Clyde asks Bonnie. "Texas, Arkansas, New Mexico, or Missouri?"

"Let the boy decide," Bonnie says.

The plates on the car are from Kansas. I know Clyde likes to change plates frequently, usually after every job.

"What'll it be, sugar?" Bonnie says to me. "You choose."

"Texas," I say with no hesitation.

"Why?"

"Because you're less likely to attract notice with in-state plates."

Bonnie steps around Clyde and kisses me on the cheek. "I think we're gonna have to recruit you. You're good-looking *and* intelligent."

She hooks her arm in mine as Clyde changes the plates.

"Why don't you go tell your father we're here," she says, almost a whisper.

"Yes, ma'am."

I quit school the previous fall to help my mother. My father had been bedridden for several months. The three of us kids—my youngest sister, Jenny, had died of diphtheria by then—would sit with him in the parlor or in his room or sometimes, when it was warm, in the backyard beneath the cherry tree when we thought he was closer to death and his fingers and toes started to lose their feeling. We just stared at the wood plank floors or the ground, those knotholes and seams and blades of grass riveting our attention. In those early months, we feared to look at him, afraid of what bad luck had done. It felt like an apology in our home. None of us knew what to say or how to express the sadness that lay like sharp stones in our stomachs, none of us looking up because what we'd see was not him but rather that huge unworldly lump, swelling so that it seemed as if a cantaloupe had taken root under his scalp, small patches of black fuzz trying to find purchase on his skull.

He was still our father, of course, but he wasn't long for this world, and after a while, we got used to the idea. He was no longer the man we'd known. During the day, he remained fairly lucid, but at night he lost hold of whatever tethered him to us. I understood sooner, since I was the oldest, and I sat with him some nights to spell my mother. It was spooky there with him, especially when he'd mutter and shout in some strange gibberish, waking me from a fitful dream of my own. He'd startle, the kerosene lamp by his bedside just barely going, and then carry on a conversation with me, as if nothing had happened, though it wouldn't be me he'd be talking to but rather his own father, who'd died in the Spanish-American War, or to his grandmother who raised him.

His head made shadows on the wall, lopsided shadows, and I'd listen and watch and not know what to say, afraid if I spoke, if I angered or contradicted him, then he'd be lost to us forever. It was a frightful time in my life, and I didn't think a day would ever go by that I wouldn't think about those nights with my father as he lay dying, his head expanding.

No one knew why it happened. A couple of the other farmers in town speculated he got kicked too many times by irritable mules, which was true. Others said it was because he'd gotten in a fight with Peter Cooley, from the next county over, and Cooley had hit him over the head with an iron rod. That, too, was true. Sam Fogarty, the sheriff, said it was drink because my father had bootlegged vinegary whiskey in 1931 when a series of floods and hailstorms ruined our cotton and corn, but my father was never much of a drinker himself. Ladies at my mother's church whispered that he'd gotten his just desserts for tomcatting all over the county, crawling between the sheets with any lonely sinner who'd spread her legs for a good time at the price of damnation. My father was no saint. I knew that. But I couldn't then, and didn't imagine I would ever, believe in a god that doles out punishment in that way.

Doc Melbourne thought it was water on his brain, brought on by a bad bout with a virus that fevered him on New Year's Day 1933. He predicted that the swelling would eventually recede. It didn't. A surgeon from Houston made a trip to our house because of research he was doing on brains and said what caused the swelling was something reproducing inside his head and that it couldn't be cut out. He told us it was probably cancer, but it could also be something else that had a long name with about fifteen consonants. The surgeon wrote it down, but my mother threw it away. He said he'd never seen a case like my father's, a head *erupting* (his word) so large and irregularly that the scalp had stretched thin enough to see the deformed skull. He said it would get worse. My father'd be in miserable pain, and then he would die, and what we should do was to make his last months as comfortable as possible.

"And make your peace with him."

"You a preacher as well as a surgeon?" my mother asked, her left eyebrow arching.

"No, ma'am," he said. "Just encouraging you to do right by him and yourselves, so you don't regret it later."

"You just take care of the diagnosing," she said. "Since you're so good at it. And we'll take care of the peacemaking."

"No offense, ma'am."

"None taken," she said, but it was clear to even those of us who weren't brain surgeons that she didn't mean it.

The only thing keeping my father halfway interested in life during this time was the newspaper stories of the Barrow Gang. He hadn't seen Clyde in more than a decade, not since Clyde was a kid. Even before my father fell ill, we were keeping track of what was happening to Clyde, his brother Buck, Bonnie, and the various members of the Barrow Gang. My father enjoyed his connection to these celebrities, and celebrities they were, even if notorious. My mother didn't approve, though she didn't want to badmouth them either. She told Whit, Clara, and me that we shouldn't brag to our friends about being related to them. That would only result in Sheriff Fogarty getting suspicious about us. Nobody wanted that, she said. Life was difficult enough.

By the summer of 1933, my father had already gotten so bad off we could sense that it wouldn't be long, excepting a miracle, before he'd be dead. So my mother let me and Whit read the newspaper stories to him while she and Clara made dinner. She thought Clara was too young for the stories and couldn't be trusted not to tell her schoolmates.

Of course, I'd learned to read before I quit school, was a damn fine reader in fact, poring over the few books we owned, including the collected works of John Milton, though my mother didn't appreciate his depiction of Satan as a seductive orator. She said it wasn't right that Satan turned out to be the most entertaining character in the book.

My father laughed. "God loves the virtuous," he said, "but everyone else loves a sinner. Even old blind Milton." My mother smiled at that, which surprised me, given the history of their relationship and the rumors about his affairs, most of them apparently true. Perhaps she was pleased to hear that he was still capable of humor, that some semblance of his former self had not been totally eclipsed by his illness.

I'd walk the couple of miles into town, or if my mother needed groceries, I'd drive the Ford and get the papers and read aloud to him about Bonnie and Clyde's latest escapades. In late July, we heard the news about Buck Barrow's grisly killing, and my father listened carefully and then reminisced about Buck, who he called Ivy, and how awful sad it was to hear about his death. He made my mother send Clyde's parents a condolence card. He wrote on it himself, in a barely legible scrawl:

Dear Cousins,

I know you ain't heard from me in a long time. I've been bad off and nobody except me thinks I'll make it much longer. I read about poor Ivy's death and I am sorry for him and for you. We follow Clyde and Miss Parker in the papers. And, good or bad, we root for our kin. Me and mine are thinking about you in your grief.

Yours,
Zachary

Miraculously, my father didn't die as soon as everybody expected. Whatever was growing inside his brain stopped for a time. His head didn't get any smaller, but it didn't get any bigger either, and there were whole weeks when he seemed almost normal again, though he still couldn't work and spent most days sleeping.

When there wasn't any news in the papers about the Barrow Gang, my father would ask us to read from the clippings that Whit and I saved in an album. We memorized the more colorful ones and would recite them with a melodramatic flourish that delighted him. He'd close his eyes, and his enormous head would swivel on his neck. His lips would part, revealing the gap between his front teeth. Whit and I would grab brooms and pretend they were BARs, acting out the Barrow Gang exploits, even as our mother, clanging her pots in the kitchen, indulged our shows before calling us to dinner, where she said the blessing, never once offering a word of prayer for our father's doomed cousin.

That was how we passed the fall and then winter and then most of the next spring, watching my father and his cousin continue to elude the forces determined to kill them off.

He's awake when I enter his room and asks, before I can say a word, "Who's here?"

"You ain't gonna believe it," I tell him and turn off the Victrola.

"Ralph?"

Ralph lives in Honey Grove and comes out every couple of weeks to check on us, usually toting a basket of vegetables or beef tips for stew. He knows money is tight with only me, my mother, and Whit doing the farming, and my mother picking up a little extra as a seamstress.

"Nope," I say. "Clyde."

He seems momentarily befuddled. "I don't know no Clyde."

"Clyde Barrow."

And then it dawns on him, but I can see, in the tightness of his lips, his confusion turn to suspicion. "Don't be funning me, Riley."

"I'm not. Clyde and Bonnie Parker are in the backyard right now. I just helped them put their car away."

"You best not be lying," he says, but I can see he's excited by the possibility. Despite the bad night of sleep, this might be a clear-headed day. His eyes aren't as rheumy as usual. I help him up and into his overalls and slippers, and then I place him in the makeshift wheelchair that Whit and I jerry-rigged by hammering wheels to one of the kitchen chairs. I roll him across the hardwood floor through the kitchen, squeeze the chair through the back door, and down the ramp we also made because he likes to be in the yard whenever it's warm enough.

"If it ain't Uncle Zach in the flesh," Clyde says.

"I thought you were cousins?"

"Well, your father's the same age as my mother, and they was as close as brother and sister, so we always called him uncle."

"Truth is," my father says, "your mother and me was kissing cousins."

"You shitting me?"

"When me and her was kids no older than my boy here, we used to sneak down by the lake in Honey Grove and ... well, I better not say what exactly we done."

"My dad know that?"

"Your father was my best friend. Used to play baseball. I'm the one that introduced him to your mother. Before long they was married and popping out you kids faster than we could keep count. How many of you are there now?"

"Eight," Clyde says.

"Which one are you again?"

"Five."

"I remember coming to see y'all when you was living under the viaduct. A damn pitiful sight. I talked to that man who owned the Star gas station, out there on Eagle Ford Road, and got Henry a job. It was still pathetic to see y'all cramped in that storage room with them Dr Pepper and Nehi signs."

"It beat the hell out of the viaduct," Clyde says and scratches at his nose. "You're right, though. Those were some glum-ass days. I remember you used to bring us some groceries and milk and play rummy with me and Buck. We ain't never forgot it either, Uncle Zach."

"How's Ivy?" my father asks. He's forgotten the articles I read to him last July, not to mention the card we sent after Buck died, the card that has no doubt prompted this visit. I thought my father would never forget the details about Buck's killing since he knew a thing or two about disfigured heads. But this slip reminds me that, even though this is a good day for him, you can never speculate accurately about what he will or won't remember, or even if he'll know you from one minute to the next.

Clyde starts to speak but then buttons up. His lips twitch. "Excuse me," he says and limps over to the side of the barn.

Bonnie watches Clyde, trying to gauge his mood, and then she reaches over and places her little hand on my father's forearm. "I'm afraid Ivy's passed away," she says.

"How'd that happen?" my father asks. "He was always a strapping boy, the laughingest sumbitch."

"I'm afraid it wasn't too pretty, sir. It was about the worst thing I ever saw in my life. And Clyde feels he's to blame."

"Well," my father says, "there's always somebody to blame for something." Bonnie flinches at what seems like my father's casual indictment.

Clyde limps back over, frowning.

My father says, "Don't let it eat you up, son."

"Can I ask you a question?" Clyde says, and I sense something ugly's about to happen.

"Shoot."

"What the hell happened to your fucking head?"

I step back. Bonnie's surprised, too, but she's undoubtedly seen this shift in Clyde before. She shakes her head slightly, as if to warn him off, and then puts her hand on his shoulder, a secret communication between them. I figure Clyde blames my father for not knowing what everyone else in the country knows, and now he wants to return the favor of an inappropriate question. I worry at this moment that his famous temper will erupt. I watch his twitchy lips. I watch his hand to see if it moves to the gun.

"Ate too many goddamn watermelon seeds," my father says.

We all stare, dumbstruck, at him. Is this my old joking father, before the swelling, or the new, frequently addled one who will say something like this, believing it himself?

There is a shocked silence, and then Clyde and Bonnie explode into laughter. My father laughs, too, a big belly laugh. I still don't know if he meant it as a joke, but it's clear he loves the good humor of the moment and the fact that he's apparently caused it. His wide-gapped teeth and the tops of his pink gums reveal themselves like a happy banner. I can't tell you how relieved and delighted I am to see that face.

For the next few minutes, the four of us give ourselves over to an all-out giggle fit. Bonnie laughs so hard that she drops down on the grass and rolls around onto her side. Clyde is just as bad, his big ears turning red, his boy's face streaming with tears. He can't catch his breath and hops around on the grass like he's eaten a bunch of Mexican jumping beans. It's the funniest thing I've ever seen in my life.

"Clyde, you look like a goddamn grasshopper," my father says.

After we regain control of ourselves, my father sends me inside for lemonade. As I make a pitcher and stare out the window at the three of them, I think it would be a good idea to show them our album of clippings, let them know the significant role they've played in the life of our family. I flip it open randomly to the page with the newspaper photo of Buck, blind-folded, on his knees, and a caption that proclaims: "One Barrow Brother Down, One to Go." It spooks me that I open it to this page, and I'm reminded that what has most fascinated me this past year has not been the details of their escapes but the possibility of their deaths. I've expected each day to see their mangled bodies on the cover of the paper when I go to town. Staring at the clipping of Buck in the album, I realize I've been hoping that they will be murdered, that their ending will not be anticlimactic, with a capture and a prolonged trial, but bloody and grand instead. I realize, too, that my feelings about Clyde and Bonnie are mixed up with my unacknowledged wish that my father will die soon to relieve us of the burden of caring for him. I feel ashamed at this moment and close the album and put it back in the drawer, returning to the kitchen to finish the lemonade.

When I come back out with the tray of glasses and the pitcher, Clyde has his shirt off, showing my father the bullet wounds on his arms and chest.

"Go ahead and touch 'em if you want," he says, and my father does, running his fingers over the raised welts.

"Ouch!" Clyde screams. My father jerks his hand away, and Clyde giggles. "I'm just kidding. It don't hurt none now."

He sits down on the chair by my father and pulls off one of his wingtip shoes and a black, threadbare sock, revealing three toes and two little stubs where his big toe and second toe should be.

"See that?" he says. "I sliced those bastards off with an ax when I was down in Eastham. Got Governor Sterling, that gullible jackass, to sign my parole."

Clyde plops his foot in my father's lap, and my father runs his fingers over the striated ridges of Clyde's missing toes. My father doesn't have much feeling left in that hand, but I wonder if there might be magic in Clyde's stubs, because my father seems to respond pleasurably to what he touches.

"Hey, Bonnie, hike up your skirt."

"No, Clyde."

"Come on now, honey." He turns to my father and me. "She nearly burned to death up in Wellington. A bridge wasn't where we thought it was, and we went right into the ravine. We barely got Bonnie away before the whole goddamn engine exploded. Cut her knee clear to the bone and burned up the prettiest thigh this side of the Ziegfeld Follies."

Reluctantly at first, Bonnie places her foot on my father's wheelchair and unwraps the gauze, shows us the gash she suffered almost a year ago. My father and Clyde oohh and aahh, and she gets into the act and hikes up her dress even more, enough to reveal her lacy peach undergarments. She shows us her thigh.

"Ain't that a beaut?" Clyde says, touching around the edges. The skin is shriveled, oily from some kind of ointment. "Hell, I think it's gonna be prettier than before," Clyde adds.

"I like a woman with battle scars," my father says, which makes Bonnie smile and Clyde giggle again. I can't get over the comedian my father's suddenly become.

"You know what we need?" Clyde asks. "A photograph. To commemorate this family reunion and show off everybody's war wounds. I know my mother would love a picture of us with her old kissing cousin."

"That sounds grand," Bonnie says.

"Son, would you go to the car and fetch the camera from the backseat? Be careful with it."

"Yes, sir," I say and race to the barn to find the Kodak box camera that they've used to take all the famous pictures of themselves—my favorite being the one where Bonnie, a cigar bobbing from her lips, holds a pistol and props her leg against one of their stolen cars. I carry the camera delicately to the front porch. I feel uneasy about having the picture taken since we haven't had any made since my father got sick. If my mother were here, she'd not allow it. She'll be showing up pretty soon, and that worries me. But she isn't here yet, and I like the idea not only of the photograph but also of me as the photographer. I entertain the fantasy that the picture might make it into the newspaper and that I will be the one to bring it home for my father.

Bonnie shows me how to take the picture, and then she and Clyde pose on either side of my father—Bonnie with her dress hiked up, revealing her wounded leg, her elbow propped on my father's shoulder, the deformed part of his head glistening in the sun. Through the lens of the camera, she seems so tiny next to my father, and I have the odd feeling he might pick her up with one hand and make her talk like a ventriloquist's dummy. Clyde sits on a stool next to my father with just his undershirt on. He thrusts his bullet-scarred arm toward the camera. His three-toed foot is propped on my father's lap.

"Smile," I say. Clyde and Bonnie remain solemn-faced, as their custom has been in photographs. My father, however, offers me that fat, gap-toothed grin of his.

Afterward, Bonnie leans over and lightly kisses my father's cheek. It's such a sweet gesture that I wish I'd had the wherewithal to take a photograph of that as well.

Clyde tells me to put the camera away, which disappoints me since I'd hoped to have my photograph taken with them, too, though I realize my father wouldn't be able to operate the camera. When I get back, Clyde has lit up a couple of cigars for himself and my father. I expect Bonnie to smoke one, too, as she did in the famous picture.

"They sour my stomach," she says, as if reading my mind. "I wish Clyde would quit the nasty habit. They stink to high heaven."

"We read the poem you wrote," I say as I pour the nearly forgotten lemonade into the glasses. I've hardly spoken a word and want to offer something to the conversation. Bonnie's poem has been reprinted in newspapers across the country.

"He can recite it from memory," my father says, and both Clyde and Bonnie seem genuinely impressed.

"A command performance," she shouts, raising her arm high. I'm eager to do it, though nervous that I might forget a line or skip a whole verse. I do well, though, and am especially dramatic, gunning an imaginary BAR as I recite my favorite lines:

> *If they try to act like citizens*
> *And rent a nice little flat*
> *About the third night they're invited to fight*
> *By a sub-gun's rat-a-tat-tat.*

They applaud enthusiastically, my father included, and I take a ceremonial bow. Then Bonnie jumps up, cups my cheeks between her hands, and kisses me on the lips. She holds the kiss until I can feel the heat rise in my face.

"Hey there, hoss, slow down a little!" Clyde jokes. "She ain't your kissing cousin."

. . .

Just after noon, my mother drives up and parks the Ford beneath the shade of the willow tree that whispers against my shutters late at night. My brother and sister bolt from the car and then stop short when they see we have guests.

"Who are you?" Clara asks.

"I'm your dad's kin," Clyde says. "Me and him go way back. You're my cousin, thrice removed," he adds, the same thing he said to me when I first met him, and I wonder if this is a phrase he's rehearsed. He seems to delight in the formality of it. "Pleased to meet ya, cuz."

Clyde shakes my sister's and then Whit's hand. I can tell by Whit's silence, the pallor of his skin, and his bug-eyed look that he recognizes them.

"You seen me before, haven't you?" Clyde asks Whit.

"No, sir."

"Seen my picture, though?"

"Yes, sir."

"So you know who I am?"

"Yes, sir."

Clyde tips his hat back on his head, smiles, and says, "Much better looking in person, ain't I?" Whit and Clara laugh.

"Don't pay him no never mind," Bonnie says.

Clyde wraps his arm around Bonnie's shoulder. "This is my wife." I wonder if they found a justice of the peace to marry them, and maybe we are the first to know it, if that is part of the reason they have come to our house, to share the news with the closest relatives.

Clara says, "Hey, Riley, you're taller than both of them, and they're grown up."

"Clara!" I shout.

Bonnie laughs, but Clyde doesn't utter a sound, which makes me wonder if the reason he set out to be a bank robber and murderer was because one too many fools made similar comments. He has a small man's chip on his shoulder.

"That's all right," Bonnie says. "What a pretty little girl." She bends down before Clara.

My mother finally appears and walks slowly toward us, a wary expression on her face. I can tell she knows who's paying us a visit.

"Hello, ma'am," Clyde says. He removes his hat and takes my mother's hand and kisses it. "Mighty pleased to meet you."

My father whistles. "Ain't he a gentleman!"

"Zachary's a cousin of mine," Clyde says. "Haven't seen him since I was a boy."

"Hello," Bonnie chirps, not waiting for an introduction. "It's an honor to make your acquaintance."

"I know who you are," my mother says flatly. She isn't rude, but it's clear that she wants to let these strangers know that she isn't a woman who can be easily charmed or fooled.

Clyde and Bonnie study my mother. The smiles drop from their faces, and then they both nod solemnly, as if they have reached a silent agreement.

"We're just making a little family call," Clyde says, though there's that edgy look in his eyes again, like when he asked my father what happened to his head.

"I suppose you'll be expecting some lunch," she says.

Clyde replaces his hat and then tips it back. "If it ain't too much trouble."

"Will stew satisfy you?" she asks, and again I sense in her question a kind of challenge, if not an insult. It makes me nervous.

"Our favorite, ma'am," Bonnie says brightly.

My mother doesn't smile back, just turns sharply and walks up the ramp into the kitchen.

Clyde says, "I don't think she likes us."

"She's just tired," I say, but of course he's right. My mother doesn't appreciate them and sure as hell doesn't appreciate them being here at our house.

"Riley, you come on and help me with lunch," my mother calls from the window. I don't want to go inside because I figure there will be an interrogation waiting for me, but I have no choice and so leave Whit and Clara with my father, Bonnie, and our famous cousin.

My mother is not old. She had me when she was seventeen, so she's barely thirty, and still pretty, though wrinkles and worry lines have etched her forehead and gathered like spiders' webs around her eyes and her lips. She does laugh sometimes, especially when she listens to the comedy routines on the radio or when we play dominoes or Wahoo. And she told me once that she had dreams before she met my father of singing on the radio. But now she only sings with the Honey Grove First Methodist choir on Sunday mornings.

"How long they been here?" my mother asks as soon as I enter the kitchen.

As she stirs the stew she began this morning before she left, and as she puts cornbread in the oven, I narrate what transpired while she was at church, leaving out the photograph. I look out the window every chance I get to see what's going on out there. Clyde does a juggling trick and then limps to his car and retrieves a couple of guns—a rifle and one of the BARs. He shows them to my father, Whit, and Clara. He even lets Whit hold the automatic. And then Bonnie seems to defend Clara's right to hold a gun as well, because she pulls out a small revolver from her purse and puts it in my sister's hand and stands behind her and helps her aim it at the cornfields. Bonnie isn't much bigger than Clara, who is only ten. The gun goes off, and Clara recoils into Bonnie, and they both stumble and nearly topple over. My mother slams the spoon into the big pot, rushes to the porch, and shouts, "Clara, you and Whit get on in here!"

"It's all right, ma'am," Clyde says. "Bonnie knows what she's doing. I taught her myself."

"They're just having fun," my father calls back.

My mother stands there on the porch for a few seconds, wondering, I believe, if she should contradict her husband in front of his relatives. Ever since he's been sick, she's been in charge. Her word is law now, but I know she doesn't want to embarrass my father. She returns to the kitchen, and I can see Whit and Clara coming along after her. They know better than to disobey her. My mother clangs some pots and scowls.

"It's okay," I offer.

"Go wash up and get that table set," she says to Whit and Clara as they slink in the kitchen door.

"They ain't gonna hurt us," I say. "We're family."

She wheels on me, the dripping spoon extended from her hand like a weapon. "No," she growls. "*We* are family."

I bow my head, more afraid at this moment of her than the criminals outside.

A few minutes later, Bonnie stands at the entrance to the kitchen. "Here, ma'am," she says, holding out an envelope. "Clyde and me'd like you to have this. We know you could use it. It's almost three hundred and fifty dollars. I'm sure it will come in handy."

Bonnie steps toward my mother, and the difference in their sizes startles me. I never think of my mother as a large woman, though four children have made her thick through the waist. I am already several inches taller than she is and outweigh her by thirty pounds. But next to Bonnie, she seems suddenly huge—looming above her. My mother keeps her hands by her side and shakes her head.

"Please, ma'am. Clyde'll be awful hurt if you refuse."

"I can't take that money."

"I understand what you're thinking," Bonnie says, brushing back a strand of reddish-blonde hair from her forehead. "You're thinking this money's tainted. But you're wrong. Money's just a thing. And the way we figure it, the reason we got this money is so we can give it to folks who really need it."

"I appreciate the gesture," my mother says.

Her mouth is set so that it's clear, to me at least, that she doesn't appreciate it but is trying to be polite. Regardless, this is a lot of money, a fortune for people like us. I wonder if this is the time to be principled.

"I can't take that money," she says again.

Bonnie squints at my mother and then, after a few moments, nods. She returns to the backyard. As my mother stirs her stew, I watch through the window as Bonnie whispers into Clyde's ear. He shakes his head and says something, and then she gives him the envelope. Bonnie kneels by my father's chair and starts to talk to him as Clyde limps onto the porch. He raps lightly on the door, which is polite but not really necessary.

"Mind if I talk to you for a moment, ma'am?"

"Come on in," my mother says, pulling the cornbread from the oven.

Clyde winks at me, as if we're allies. I want to be.

"I gotta ask you a favor."

Without looking at him, my mother says, "I'm not taking it." Clyde silently watches her as she cuts the cornbread with a long knife and puts the pieces in a bowl. When she finishes, she says, "And if you're worried that I'm gonna call the police as soon as you leave, then I can assure you that won't happen. Whatever you've done, you're still Zachary's kin."

I suddenly notice that it's gotten real quiet in the dining room. Whit and Clara must be listening, too.

"I'm much obliged, ma'am. But the favor I'm asking ain't for me. I understand why you got some qualms about how we got this money. But you've got a hard time coming your way. Your kids are a help, but they ain't a man. And by the looks of things, that hard time is coming soon."

"You don't have to talk in riddles," my mother says. "The boy knows his father will die. We all know it. He's lived longer, as it is, than anyone expected. I appreciate your gesture, Mr. Barrow. But if I take that envelope, and I use what's in it, then I'm no better than a thief myself. That money, you and I both know, has blood on it."

Clyde stares down at his dust-covered wingtips and collects his thoughts before proceeding.

"This favor ain't for me. My mother, she loved Zachary like he was her brother. She asked me to come here, asked me to give you this money. He helped us when we was desperate, and he always treated us like we wasn't trash. She never forgot it. Me neither. I ain't a Christian, ma'am. I 'spect you know that. I figure when I'm dead, I'm gone, and the maggots can have me. If there's a heaven and a hell, then I'm sure we both know where I'll be headed. But this gift ain't from me. It's from my mother. She asked that I do this. And I want to grant her that wish. I've brought enough grief on her as it is."

My mother listens to this speech calmly and seems to take it seriously. I stand at the stove, holding my breath, hoping they won't send me out. She wipes her hands on her apron.

After a few moments, she says, her voice warmer now, "I'm sorry, Mr. Barrow. I just can't do that. If it'd ease your mind, you tell your mother that you made good on your promise. I won't naysay you, if it comes to it. But I can't have that money in my house, no matter what good purpose we might put it to. I hope you'll understand and appreciate that and not hold it against me or my husband."

Clyde stares at my mother. He seems like a sheepish boy who's been scolded, though my mother has not raised her voice, and her last words have been as much a plea as a statement of resolve. He nods, as Bonnie did, and puts the envelope in his pocket.

"Would it trouble you too much if we spent the night? We would sleep in the barn."

She examines Clyde's face carefully for a few seconds and seems to weigh what she wants to tell him. "I'm happy to feed you a meal."

This seems to stun Clyde more than her refusal of the money. I wonder how long it has been since someone refused him not only one request but two.

"Yes, ma'am," he says and puts his hat back on his head. "Sorry to trouble you. We'll be heading out soon."

He touches the brim with his finger in a kind of salute to my mother, and then smiles grimly at me before walking out the door.

I start to say something to her but then stop, not sure what it is I have to tell her. I can't quite believe what I've seen her do, nor the deference that both Clyde and Bonnie have shown her. I admire her, even if I disagree with her. I know we need that money.

"Go bring your father inside."

"But—"

"You heard me," she says and then begins ladling the stew into bowls.

"We gotta be heading out," Clyde is telling my father as I come outside.

"So soon?" my father asks, genuinely surprised. "I thought you was spending the night. We've plenty of room."

"I'm afraid not. Gotta get to Bonnie's mother's house in West Dallas by nightfall."

"Stay for dinner at least."

"I wish we could," Bonnie says. "But we gotta go. My momma will have herself a hissy fit if I'm late." I know the lie of this. Policemen are staked out permanently at the Parker and Barrow households. This isn't conjecture on my part. The papers have said as much.

Bonnie leans over and kisses my father's cheek, and then, in a gesture I will never forget, she kisses him on the bad side of his head. It's gentle, and she lingers there. It seems to me like a blessing. And then they are gone.

A few weeks later, the radio buzzes with the news of the deaths of Clyde Barrow and Bonnie Parker. They were ambushed and slaughtered in Black Lake, Louisiana, their car and bodies riddled with bullets by police.

My father sends me to town to fetch the paper, which proclaims, "Infamous Duo Finally Get Their Due," and tells the gory details of the ambush. Their bodies are being delivered to Dallas, where they will be on public display before the funeral.

"Go see them off, son," my father says when I finish reading him the article. "Your cousin ought to have as much family there as he can."

My father is adamant. My mother, surprisingly, relents without argument and fills a basket with sausage, pickles, cold potato patties, and a thermos of sweet tea for me and Whit. She lets me drive the Ford. Though I drive a lot on the farm and in town, it is the first time I'm being allowed to drive in a city. We're to stay with her sister in Fort Worth.

Rumors fly in Dallas. We hear that in Louisiana, where they were shot, people tore off bits of Clyde's and Bonnie's clothing as trophies and that someone even tried to cut off Clyde's ear. We hear that a photographer has taken a picture of their naked, mangled bodies, and that it's circulating at the funeral, though I don't see it and know I will tear it up if I do. We hear that someone stole Clyde's diamond stickpin from his jacket, though I doubt that. Clyde didn't have a stickpin on his jacket. I remember everything about him.

Their bodies, still bloody, are put on display in Dallas. Hot dog vendors set up stands on every corner, and kids sell iced Nehis and Dr Peppers to the folks waiting in line in the heat to catch a glimpse. A couple standing in front of us says that a man offered $50,000 for Clyde's body so that he could mummify it and take it on tour. I notice that some of the people—kids you might expect, but also a man and an old woman—are touching them, rubbing their handkerchiefs over my cousin and Bonnie.

"Goddamn it," I mutter to Whit. "I wish I could shoot those sons of bitches."

But when I file past, I touch Clyde's hand as well and then pluck a strand of hair from Bonnie's skull.

"What are you doing?" Whit shouts when I show him. "You want to bring us bad luck?" Whit will steal the hair from me that night and bury it in our aunt's yard.

I will read later that almost twenty thousand people filed past their bodies.

Clyde and Bonnie have separate funerals, which makes me sad since that isn't the way they wanted it, not the way Bonnie foretold it in her poem. We go to Clyde's funeral, since he is kin, and squeeze with so many others into the old Belo Mansion on Ross Avenue, which has been converted into a funeral home.

At the gravesite, we can't get in close enough to see Clyde's coffin, even when we say we're family.

"Who ain't?" a policeman snarls and then pushes Whit and me back with his nightstick.

Clyde's parents look too old to be of my father's generation, but maybe their boys have aged them. They are nearly knocked into the grave when an airplane suddenly drops an enormous wreath on Clyde's coffin. We will learn later that the famous racketeer Benny Binion hired the plane. "Binion's Bouquet Bomb," the Dallas paper calls it.

When Whit and I arrive home, my father is already dead. My mother says he died on May 26, in the afternoon, at almost three o'clock, the day of Clyde's funeral. I think about where I was at that moment and realize Whit and I were at the gravesite. I close my eyes and imagine it, the two images superimposed over each other, the bouquet bomb dropping from the low-flying plane as my father exhales his last breath.

Maybe that's just wishful thinking on my part, but there doesn't seem any harm in believing it, though I don't mention this to my mother, who I know might have a different interpretation. I don't want my father dead, and I am sorry I wasn't there for his final hours, but a part of me feels it's appropriate he died the day they buried Clyde and Bonnie. They had, in a peculiar way, been keeping him alive.

About a week after we bury him, we get a letter. It's postmarked from Louisiana and addressed to my father. My mother opens it up, and inside are a little card, a newspaper clipping, and a photograph. The card says:

> Thanks for your hospitality. I sure do hope you're feeling better, Zachary. Enclosed please find an autographed copy of the poem your son recited so brilliantly. I never had a better compliment in my life. Also please find the photograph he took of us. It's a splendid one, I think. Clyde especially likes your hairdo and his toes. See the inscription.

The picture is the one I'd taken, of course, with their Kodak box camera. Bonnie with her skirt hiked up to show her scar, her elbow resting on my father's shoulder. Clyde sitting on the stool with his shoe and sock off and his three-toed foot draped across my father's lap. Just my father smiling. A falling cherry blossom from the tree suspended above my father's head. On the back of the photo, in Bonnie's girlish cursive: "The Barrow Gang Displays Their Scars."

Bonnie must have sent it from a post office in Louisiana not long before they died. It feels strange to me—to all of us, really—to be getting a letter and a photograph from the dead.

At the sight of the picture, my mother sits down at the table and starts to weep so hard that she has to rest her head in her hands. She's not a weeper, so this surprises and moves me so much that I start to cry as well. She drops the picture to the floor, and I pick it up.

"Give me that," she orders, and I hand it to her. She wipes her eyes and then tears the picture in two. "That's not the way we're gonna remember him," she says. "With some two-bit…." She stops herself and takes a deep breath. "…. and her murdering boyfriend making fun of him, making fun of us all."

She stands up, drops the two pieces in the trashcan. "It was all just a lark to them," she says. And then she goes back to her room and lies down on her bed. She doesn't get up for three days.

I retrieve the torn pieces. The rip is precisely through the middle of my father's face, right between his eyes. On one piece of the photo is the bad part of his head, with Bonnie by his side. Clyde's bare, three-toed foot is on that side as well. On the other piece is the normal part of my father's head. Our cousin Clyde sitting beside him, his leg draped across my father's lap. I am intrigued by the precision of my mother's rip. I don't know why, but it seems to me like a signal from the other side, some indication that they might be all right, though I know that such a thought would make them laugh. I keep the two parts of that photograph, hide it in our copy of Milton because I know my mother won't open it. I later tape it together, but you can still see the crease through my father's head, face, and body, as well as the suspended cherry blossom.

Far from ruining the picture, it makes it better.

Sometimes I pull out that picture, still lodged all these decades later between the pages of our old copy of *Paradise Lost*, a fitting place for it, I think. It's the first picture I ever took—and the best one as well. And it's the only one I have of my father. I marvel now at how young he looks, despite the grotesque evidence of his illness and only weeks before his death.

I'm now more than twice the age he was then.

I like to imagine sometimes that I'm in that picture with them, standing behind the three of them, just off to my father's good side. It's a photograph that I could have sold for a lot of money if I'd wanted to. But I never did, not even during the worst years for us, not even after the famous movie came out and it might have fetched a good price.

As I've recounted this event, I've been debating with myself if I should tell the other part, the missing part that I've not told anyone since it happened—not Whit, not Clara, not my mother, nor my children or grandchildren, who have heard this story dozens of times over the years. Certainly not my wife, who passed more than a decade ago. The missing part can't, in the long run, change anything now, though I've hoped it would just disappear with all the other tellings, like an itchy scab that might shrivel and fall away if I stopped picking at it. I'm realizing it will stop haunting me only if I go ahead and tell it, put this part back in the story.

That day, after Bonnie kisses my father, after she blesses him, she and Clyde do not immediately leave. Clyde shakes my father's hand and tells him to take care of himself and stay away from the moonshine, and then he beckons me to help him with the barn doors.

I follow him. Bonnie walks beside me and again hooks her arm in mine. Inside the barn, she kisses me lightly on the cheeks, and I'm disappointed that it's not on the lips like before.

"You take good care of your mother and daddy," she says.

They get in their car, and Clyde starts the engine. He waves me over to his window and slips the envelope inside the bib pocket of my overalls.

"I can't," I protest, stealing a glance out the barn door across the backyard, where my father still sits in his wheelchair, waiting for me to roll him inside, to the kitchen window, where I know my mother is watching, though I cannot see her because of the sun glinting off the glass.

"Your mother's a good woman," Clyde says. "I admire that. But I have a good mother, too. This money belongs to your family. You're the oldest. You don't have to tell her. Just keep it safe and use it how you see fit."

"I can't."

"Please, sugar," Bonnie coos, leaning over in the seat. "It's for the best."

I don't say yes, but I don't protest anymore, and all three of us know that my refusal to say anything is really my answer.

"Watch for us in the newspapers," Clyde says.

"I will."

"You a praying man?" Bonnie asks.

"I guess."

"Well," she says, "don't waste your prayers on us."

Clyde smiles, touches the brim of his hat with his finger in another ironic salute, and then eases the car out of the barn and around the path alongside the house, past our Ford. Then he guns the engine in a gesture that I feel is intended for my mother.

"He sure was a short feller," my father says when I rejoin him. "Don't look like he growed up much since I last saw him."

Though we are on the backside of the house, I see the plume of dust from their stolen sedan billowing over our roof like a tornado.

"Dinner ready yet?" my father asks.

"I believe so," I say and then wheel him up the ramp and into my mother's kitchen.

And what became of that money? I hid it under a loose floorboard beneath my bed. I spent a little on a new Kodak camera for myself, the same model that Clyde and Bonnie owned. I took pictures with it for the next four decades, and I still own it, though it no longer works.

I used seventy dollars to pay for Whit's funeral and another seventy for Clara's. Both of them died when an influenza epidemic swept through Honey Grove in 1938. The rest I gave to the bank that same year for back taxes and mortgage, but it wasn't enough to stop the foreclosure a year later.

I never told my mother about the money, and I don't think she suspected, though I could never be sure what she saw or didn't see through the kitchen window when I stood in the cool darkness of the barn and said my goodbyes to Clyde and Bonnie. There were times when she looked at me in a way that made me wonder if she knew about the money, and there were other times when I wondered if she had refused their offer because she knew full well that they'd give it to me. I picked up extra work at the welding shop in town, and she never asked too many questions.

For a while, I believed Bonnie's argument that money didn't have a moral value, was simply paper to be used for exchange. Money could not carry the sins of its acquisition or the ghosts of those who'd died for it. But with my father dying on the day of their funerals, at the very moment that the flowers from the sky nearly crushed the onlookers, with Whit and then Clara dying, and then us losing the farm, I began to wonder if my mother was right. But it was too late to do anything about it by then.

I hope she went to her grave without knowing that the money from my famous cousin had tainted our family, after all, despite her efforts to avoid it. During her final moments, I came close to telling her what I'd done, but the more I considered it, the crueler that seemed. To tell her would have been merely to unburden my own guilt on a woman who needed no other burdens.

The Man Who Fell from the Sky

On New Year's Eve morning, 1962, Neil and Ben Brewer tossed a duffel bag of clothes and Uncle Jimmy's binoculars into the back of Neil's truck.

"You boys be careful," their mother said. "Neil, you watch out for Ben." She brushed their hair back and straightened their jackets and double-checked the basket she had packed with turkey and ham sandwiches, four big pickles, several cobs of corn, a pan of walnut brownies, and a large thermos of coffee. "I know you boys love your Uncle Jimmy," she said, "and I know he told you where you could get into the most trouble. But don't go tomcatting all over Dallas and wind up in jail. If you do, your father and me ain't coming to get you. You understand?"

They nodded and kissed her, and then Harvey Lee (they'd always called him Harvey Lee rather than Dad or Pop) shook their hands and winked at them, and they headed out of the snow-lined driveway of the farm for the five-hour drive to Dallas.

Neil was twenty and Ben seventeen. It was the first time Neil had been out of Oklahoma since he traveled with his senior class to Washington, D.C. Ben couldn't remember when he was last out of the state, and they spent the first half-hour of the trip pondering this conundrum, recounting every one of Ben's seventeen years before coming to the conclusion that Ben had never left Oklahoma, not even as a baby, had hardly even been outside the county. How sad was that?

Both of them were tall and rangy, though Neil had muscled up since he graduated because he'd been working full-time on the family's farm in Reed and gotten extra work hauling bags of grain to and from the silos in Altus. He had black, straight hair that oiled when it grew too long, and his ears stuck out when he was a teenager, but now his face had transformed into something approaching handsomeness. Happy that school was behind him, he had no intention of going to college, couldn't see the point. His favorite joke was that he'd graduated in the top ten of his class, the punch line being that there were only nine seniors the year he graduated. He did miss playing basketball and football for teams pulled together from all the little schools in Greer County. He'd had a few girlfriends—mainly summer flings at Quartz Mountain Lake with rich gals from Oklahoma City or Tulsa—and even one Spanish girl whose father was a visiting engineering professor at Kansas State University. He'd fumbled through the loss of his virginity with her late one night in the cab of his truck as she whispered a rosary in Spanish, and then she left for Manhattan, Kansas, the next day, and he never heard from her again.

Though Neil had not done that well in school, he was bright and funny and quick on his feet, and everyone figured he'd go off—to Oklahoma State or maybe the University of Texas—so there was a sense of palpable disappointment that he'd hung about for the last year and a half, still living with his folks on the farm, still farting around Greer County. But he seemed, in general, oblivious to this disappointment, and felt in fact a lightness, especially driving home from Altus, his body caked in sweat and dust, the cool night breeze blowing over his skin, the taste of a hand-rolled cigarette in his mouth, the thought of the weekend and the almost criminal pleasure of being able to watch women in their bikinis baking on the makeshift beach by the lake, or dreaming illicitly of his Aunt Doris, who was about the sexiest goddamn woman he'd ever seen.

Ben was the brilliant one, or so everyone said, including Ben. He liked to read novels and poetry and could quote all of "The Charge of the Light Brigade" and long passages from Shakespeare's *Henry IV, Part 1*—*Banish plump Jack, and banish all the world!*—and Shakespeare's sonnet about his ugly mistress with her reeking breath and dun-colored breasts, clomping around like an old ugly hag rather than some angel on a pedestal. And the other one that Ben and Neil referred to as the sugar daddy sonnet:

> *When my love swears that she is made of truth*
> *I do believe her, though I know she lies that*
> *She might think me some untutored youth*
> *Unlearned in the world's false subtleties.*

Ben was also good with numbers, so good that he had surpassed his teachers' skills by the time he was in sixth grade. In high school, he had to send off for trigonometry and calculus books. In his sophomore year, Ben had grown ten inches. He was so skinny now, his ribs poking obscenely through the skin, that Harvey Lee said he looked like a piece of vanilla taffy God had stretched lengthwise. He had blond hair with a stubborn cowlick and thick, black-framed glasses, and a face full of freckles. He could play most anything on the piano, had a smooth tenor voice, and could beat the pants off anybody in Scrabble and chess. Girls loved him, and yet Ben seemed unaware, on some level, of his own charms: shy with women, rarely even going on a date, preferring to read or work out some complex mathematical calculation rather than ogle the bikinied masterpieces at Quartz Mountain or go to the drive-in over in Altus with Neil and a couple of vacationing girls.

Neil loved Ben, not just out of brotherly devotion but because Ben was pretty damn fun to be around, even though he had his head stuck in books a lot of the time. Neil didn't even begrudge the fact that everybody believed Ben would earn a scholarship when he graduated, maybe even to an Ivy League school. The sky was the limit for Ben. Neil thought he might even wind up becoming an astronaut, orbiting through space like John Glenn, the poster boy of all astronauts with his shit-eating grin and boyish blond crew-cut. The only thing Neil really worried about now was that his brother would leave in a year and a half, after he graduated, and then who the hell would he have to pal around with? Greer County wasn't that big.

On the windswept road out of Reed, south to Dallas, Neil's truck swayed back and forth. They both agreed that this trip was the best gift that Uncle Jimmy had ever given them—which was saying a lot—and then they concurred that Jimmy was probably the best damn uncle any two nephews could hope to have. They rode in silence for a while to solemnize their gratitude, and then Neil asked for one of those big pickles. After Ben rummaged around in the basket and unwrapped them from the briny wax paper, he turned on the radio and kept adjusting the knobs from town to town, trying to pick up a good rock-and-roll station, but it was hard to get anything except twangy cry-in-your-beer ballads between Wichita Falls and Fort Worth.

But they didn't care because they were going to Dallas for the historic event, and it was all because of Uncle Jimmy's (and Doris'—let's not forget Aunt Doris) generosity.

How could you not love Uncle Jimmy? Jimmy was twenty-nine, Harvey Lee's youngest brother by seventeen years. He'd served as a paratrooper in Korea, had been decorated many times, including a special commendation from General

MacArthur himself. After the Korean War ended, Jimmy traveled the world, working as a cook and bartender in New York and Los Angeles, a bouncer in a couple of brothels in Spain, a ski instructor in Austria, and even for a short while as the driver for a barbershop quartet that traveled through Italy, France, and Greece.

Just after Kennedy won the election, Jimmy returned to Greer County with beautiful Doris. Doris was just the woman you'd imagine finding in San Diego. She had long, silky blonde hair that moved like a California wave over the side of her face. She had worked for a while as a model in Los Angeles, and her lips were the lips you'd want to see in a cosmetics advertisement, as smooth and delicious as a plum. A mesmerizing kaleidoscopic green spray flecked her brown eyes. She wasn't any slouch around the house or some California complainer, either, which is what Neil and Ben's mother first suspected. She could make a lethal cherry cobbler, sprinkled with cinnamon and spiked with rum, and she could hold her own on the farm without a single whimper, expertly separating the cotton from the bolls and pulling the fruit for hours from the trees in the orchards. Her breasts and hips moved in her dress like small animals, and Neil wished he could stop himself from staring.

"You're gonna get your head knocked off," Harvey Lee said one hot afternoon last August when they were all pulling peaches from the trees. Neil had been gazing in a trance at his aunt, perched on a ladder two trees over, her arms outstretched, revealing a sliver of flesh between her arm and her startlingly white bra. "If not by her," Harvey Lee whispered, "then by Jimmy."

One thing Neil admired about Doris was that she wasn't a priss or prude whose delicate sensibilities might be upset by a cussword. Every week or so, Neil and Ben would go over to Doris and Jimmy's rented house in Mangum. She'd make a big dish of lasagna for them all, or Jimmy would grill bloody hamburgers and char some hotdogs, and Jimmy's friends would come over. They'd sit around singing, Doris playing the upright piano Jimmy had bought for thirty-five dollars. She played with a jazzy relish that Neil thought was as good as Nat King Cole, with Ben relieving her every once in a while. Jimmy and his buddies would sing in four-part harmony, and sometimes Neil and Ben joined in, but mainly they'd sit on the couch or lounge in the chairs and drink beers and listen as they got quietly drunk, grateful to be included in Doris and Jimmy's circle of friends. Doris would make margaritas sometimes, especially if one of Jimmy's friends had been down to Mexico and brought back some mescal, or they'd break out the Jack Daniels and sip the whiskey over ice until it got late, and everybody sat around the kitchen table or in the small living room, or in the summer out in the backyard where they had a picnic table, some lounge chairs, a hammock, and an inflatable pool. Jimmy and the others who'd been to Korea would tell stories, mainly about the tedium and the goddamn trench foot and the goddamn blisters and the goddamn heat, but every once in a while they'd grow nostalgically somber recalling this friend or that fool who got his ass blown sky-high by a grenade or landmine, or some poor fucker who got a bullet through the eye or had his arm burned to goo by a gasoline bomb.

Doris would lounge on the couch with her bare legs sprawled over Jimmy's lap and let her long fingers play lightly through his hair, sliding them soothingly across his tan collarbone. Late at night, with all of them sipping their drinks, Neil and Ben pulling on their warm beers, Jimmy would talk a cackling blue streak, recounting his and Doris' private history as if it were something sacred and special, worthy of constant commemoration—how they met at Waikiki Willie's in San Diego where she was working as a cocktail waitress, how he'd begged her to marry him a hundred times ("a hundred and twenty-seven times," Doris corrected) before she finally relented, how he convinced her to move back to Oklahoma last year, reversing the journey of the most famous Okies. And now Doris was working as a hostess at the Quartz Mountain Country Club and Jimmy was a park ranger at Quartz Mountain and gave water skiing lessons on the weekends in the summer and volunteered for the Greer County Fire Department.

"Why did you come back here?" Neil asked Uncle Jimmy one night, after everyone had left except Ben and him.

"There are two kinds of people," Jimmy said philosophically, leaning forward, an ash-eaten cigarette serving as a pointer, his thick black hair tied in little pigtails by Doris. "Two kinds, I tell you: restless wanderers and homesick pussies. The sooner you find out which one you are, the better. You may have to try to be one before you discover you're the other. Me, I thought I was a wanderer, but the longer I was away from here, the more I figured out I was just a pussy."

They all laughed, and Doris took a long, slow drag from her cigarette and closed her eyes, seeming to contemplate this small pleasure.

"You go out and test yourselves against the world, boys. And don't wait for a war to make you do it. You understand? I saw plenty of the world, and I prefer Reed, Oklahoma, and this little piece of paradise."

He reached his big hand over to Doris's thigh and squeezed, making her smile, even though she didn't open her eyes.

"We better get going," Neil said, sensing their cue to leave.

"Be sure and tell old Harvey Lee," Jimmy said, leaning back, "that it's a terrible injustice I got both the brains *and* the big dick."

Ben and Neil smiled. This was an old joke, something they had first heard Jimmy say long ago when they all went fishing. When Uncle Jimmy said it to Harvey Lee,

Neil and Ben—who were fourteen and eleven at the time—thought for sure their father would haul off and punch Jimmy. But Harvey Lee just laughed and shook his head, re-hooked the stink bait, and cast out his line. Now, every time Uncle Jimmy would get drunk, he'd bring up the shame and misfortune of this deficiency.

Doris said, "Oh, you shut up, you skinny bull." And then, encouragingly to Ben and Neil, she said, "It's not the size that counts anyway. It's what you can do with what you got."

"She's just trying to make you feel better, boys, because the sad truth of the matter is that you two have your father's genes and therefore suffer in comparison to your Uncle Jimmy as well. And I'm sure, Neil, that of the two of you, bookish Ben's got you beat. On both counts."

"Hush, now," Doris said, shaking her head but smiling. "Don't listen to him. It's not about size. It's about velocity and rhythm."

They all laughed, Jimmy too. Doris was from California, where women apparently talked without shame about sex. It made Neil want to go west and find his own beautiful wife with rolling hips and green-flecked eyes and a yellow wave of hair, a woman who could drink you under the table and offer practical advice about what to do with your penis if it happened to be smaller than Uncle Jimmy's. Though it wouldn't do to have a wife so pretty that every damn guy who saw her wanted to sleep with her, just as Neil fantasized about Aunt Doris—the "aunt" giving the fantasy a little extra kick.

Uncle Jimmy was a great gift-giver, even when he was away in Korea. He'd send them gold-plated chopsticks and elaborate belts with Korean characters on them and intricately decorated fans and silk kimonos (for Granny and Neil's mother), as well as some shell casings and a framed photograph of him on furlough in Japan being held naked, except for a cloth over his crotch, in the arms of six geisha girls. Five years ago, he sent Neil and Ben packages from Greece that were stuffed full of currency from all the countries he'd been to. Each package had a hundred different bills—Italian lire, English pounds, French francs—as well as twenty-five American ones. When Ben dumped his envelope, the bills fluttered like confetti in the air, and three of them flew into the fire and crinkled into black ash. It was a wonderful waste—too much, both Harvey Lee and their mother (who'd grown up and spent their frugal courtship in the shadow of the Depression) exclaimed, but they smiled when they said it, and Neil could tell his parents were as tickled by Jimmy's generosity as they were.

This past Christmas, Neil and Ben didn't expect much because Jimmy and Doris were trying to get pregnant and were saving money for the down payment on their own house. Uncle Jimmy had said for the boys not to get their hopes up. But when they opened the tiny, wrapped box, they found a fifty-dollar bill paper-clipped to two fifty-yard-line tickets for the Cotton Bowl in Dallas on New Year's Day.

"Figured you wouldn't want to miss history in the making," Jimmy said, smiling. The Texas Longhorns were undefeated, ranked fourth in the country, and had an outside shot at the national title. They were playing seventh-ranked Louisiana State and were favored to win. Neil and Ben had never been to a college game before, certainly nothing on the scale of the Cotton Bowl.

Later, Uncle Jimmy took them aside and slipped a piece of paper into Neil's palm that had the name and address of a brothel (Jimmy's term—not *cathouse*, not *whorehouse*) in Fort Worth run by a classy Irish woman, where the girls had straight teeth and were vigilant about hygiene.

"They don't even care how small your dicks are," Jimmy kidded. "Have a good time on me, boys."

Neil and Ben arrived in Dallas by the middle of the afternoon, and they spent two hours driving around in circles before they stopped and got a Dallas-Fort Worth street map. That night they went to a bar on the seedier side of Fort Worth where Uncle Jimmy had told them the fun resided, and after fueling themselves on beer, they found the brothel. The Irish lady who owned the establishment—a still-beautiful woman with a large platter of shimmering gray hair and a slender, good-postured build—wouldn't let Ben go upstairs with any of the girls. She claimed that she possessed a special arrangement with the chief of police assuring her no trouble as long as she didn't cater to minors. She let Ben play Scrabble with the girls in the lobby while Neil went upstairs with a young redhead named Marietta. Marietta inspected and washed his pecker and asked him what he wanted to do, as if he had options. He said just the normal, so she lay on the bed and opened her thighs like a book and Neil gazed stupidly, never having seen a completely naked woman in the light; the image half-nauseated him and half-thrilled him. He leapt on the bed and did what he'd paid for. It was all over much too soon, and now he was fifteen dollars poorer, but Uncle Jimmy would be happy for him.

He went downstairs. Nobody wanted Ben to leave in the middle of the Scrabble game, so Ben told Neil to use his share for a double. Neil galloped upstairs with a blonde named Gillian who reminded him of Doris. She let him lay beside her in the bed afterward, and he asked her to stroke his head with her gold-painted fingernails and tell him where she was from. It wasn't busy that night—surprising, considering it was New Year's Eve—and she wasn't used to having men show a sympathetic interest in her autobiography. She poured them both a drink from the bottle of Scotch she kept hidden in the closet and unraveled a complicated and tragic narrative including a cruel Presbyterian minister from Kentucky and a mother and sister who had died of diphtheria. Gillian proclaimed that she wasn't long for this life, and Neil wondered if she meant life in general or life in the brothel until she explained that she was working her way through the Fort Worth Beauty Academy, and then she was going to open up her own shop after she saved enough money, and then get married and have four children, three boys and one girl. Gillian had a slow Southern accent that lulled him into a sentimental reverie. Suddenly, they heard a loud shout, followed by corks popping, and then a melodious version of "Auld Lang Syne." She offered him a freebie for being so sweet and attentive, and afterward they kissed and joked about how much they adored each other.

When Neil and Gillian went back downstairs, Ben was playing the piano and singing "Danny Boy" with three of the girls, including Marietta. The Irish woman sat in the corner, crocheting a bright blue sweater.

"I'm going to have to put the timer on you again, Gillian," the Irish woman scolded, and Neil could tell there was a history of reprimand and rebellion between them. He felt fortunate to have been the recipient of what might very well be the last of Gillian's talkative indolence and good will.

They slept in the back of Neil's truck, not wanting to waste what was left of their money on a hotel room. They shivered when it dropped into the forties, nothing to keep them warm but their jackets, baseball caps, and horse blankets. They woke scratching themselves, smelling of hay and oats, then found a fifty-cent ham-and-egg diner, swilled some bad coffee to warm and wake them, checked on directions to the Cotton Bowl, and headed over.

Though Neil and Ben had grown up in Oklahoma, they had never liked the arrogant Sooners, had always rooted for the Texas Longhorns because their mother's older brother, Uncle Deeb, had been a famous running back in '40 and '41 with the Longhorns and had even been a finalist for the Heisman his junior year. Everyone had such high hopes for him, figured he was a lock to win it the following year and would eventually go to the NFL and become another Galloping Ghost or Bronko Nagurski, or even a Slingin' Sammy Baugh since he could not only run like an antelope but throw the ball seventy yards. But after the Japs bombed Pearl Harbor, he enlisted and was killed in the Pacific less than six months later. This was all ancient history. This famous uncle was dead before Neil and Ben were born, but they felt they knew him, not only because of the newspaper clippings and magazine photos their mother kept in an album in the den but because of the way she would get misty-eyed when she recalled the great thrill she, her parents, her six other brothers and sisters, and even Harvey Lee felt sitting in the stands on a Saturday afternoon with thousands of other wildly cheering fans, all decked out in the burnt orange and white of Texas, all of them holding their index fingers and pinkies up—*Hook 'em, Horns!*—all of them shouting Deeb's name again and again as he threaded his way through the slow-footed defenders or launched a beautiful, perfectly spiraling bomb to an orange-jerseyed receiver streaking toward the end zone.

This past year, Neil and Ben and their mother had listened to every Texas game they could on the radio, and they particularly relished the Longhorns' whipping of the Oklahoma Sooners. With each win, the Longhorns climbed higher in the standings until they were undefeated with just one tie and were poised, if the cards fell just right with the other New Year's Day bowls, to win their first national championship. LSU was a scary team, however, and not to be taken lightly. They had an All-American halfback, Jerry Stovall, who had already been offered a $100,000 contract by the Houston Oilers, along with a promise of a $50,000 loan to help him start a dentistry practice in Houston after his pro career. *The Dallas Morning News* reported that Billy Bidwell, the owner of the St. Louis Cardinals, would be at the game and planned to rush onto the field at the end with an even better offer to keep the All-American in the NFL rather than lose him to the upstart AFL Oilers. And the Tigers' famous Chinese Bandits defense had shut down some of the best offenses in the country, which worried Neil since Texas' offense had sputtered late in the season, despite the play of pro prospects Jerry Cook and Ray Poage. The Longhorns had relied too much on their great linebackers, Johnny Treadwell and Pat Culpepper, for key wins that preserved their undefeated record. The Longhorns were favored, but Ben, who combed through each team's statistics and had an uncanny ability to predict the outcome of games, believed that LSU would spoil Texas' season in a defensive stalemate.

When they arrived, the stadium seemed to them a magnificent feast, an enormous concrete salad bowl to be filled with seventy-five thousand people. Neil and Ben had never seen that many people in their entire lives, much less in the same place. They elbowed their way to the concession stand in the cool, shadowed walkway, bought overpriced hotdogs and beers, and then headed for the stairwell.

"Goddamn, this place is huge," Neil said. He suddenly felt insignificant, a tiny ant on a teeming hill.

Ben led the way down the concrete steps to their seats, which were so close to the field that Neil could smell the newly mowed grass, see the bald patches of dirt beneath. (The Cotton Bowl was known for thin, slick turf that turned the field into a mud bath on a rainy day.) On the sidelines, the players joked and butted helmets and tossed the ball around.

"They're only boys!" Ben said as they squeezed into their seats. He was right. Neil could see their faces, not just the black war paint beneath their eyes but the pimples on their cheeks and chins, the boyish laughter as they chucked the ball to each other. The same age as Neil, maybe just a year or two older. He and Ben had listened as the radio announcers called their names and rendered their exploits in an epic narrative, and yet now it struck Neil as absurd—and somehow wonderful—that all this hoopla was over boys playing a game.

"Can we have your attention, ladies and gentlemen," the announcer exclaimed over the speakers, his voice sounding like a god's. "Please direct your eyes to the sky."

Everyone looked up, waiting, wondering what would happen. The Texas band's horn section trumpeted and then stopped just as abruptly so that an expectant silence filled the air. A buzzing drone approached the stadium, and then a moment later two small, old-fashioned planes skimmed the stadium's lip and dipped down toward the field. One plane was painted orange and white for Texas, the other blue and yellow for LSU. The planes moved slowly, their wings almost touching. Over midfield, both planes rolled in unison, so that it appeared for a brief moment as if the pilots—who wore long, brightly colored scarves that dangled from their necks like nooses—would fall from the planes. The crowd gasped and then applauded.

"That was amazing!" Ben yelled. The noise in the stadium was so loud that Neil could only read his lips.

Moments later, a man began singing "The Star Spangled Banner," and the crowd stood and took off their hats and held their hands over their hearts and sang along. A gust of patriotism swept through Neil. After the surprisingly harmonious "land of the free and the home of the brave," two giant-sized papier-mâché mascots—a longhorn, a tiger—each attached to helium balloons, were wheeled out to the fifty-yard line. They hovered about ten feet above the field, their legs tethered to sandbags. Two men simultaneously cut the ropes, and the mascots floated up and up and up. The crowd fell silent for a strange, magical moment, and then the applause and cheers deafened Neil as everybody watched the mascots rise slowly above the crowd and disappear into the white marbled sky.

The game, once it began, seemed almost beside the point to Neil, after these pre-game miracles. The first half was, as Ben predicted, a defensive struggle. The Longhorns couldn't get anything going offensively. The LSU defenders were quick and hard-hitting and seemed literally to fly through the air like Chinese acrobats, tripping Poage in the backfield and nearly decapitating Cook in one gruesome tackle that made the hotdog in Neil's stomach flip. Everyone in the stadium expected the Tiger star, Stovall, to have a big day running, but LSU kept passing instead.

"What's going on?" Ben asked. "The Tigers only completed forty passes all year."

LSU looked like the best team through the first two quarters, alternating their quarterbacks, the balls launched beautifully. Neil hailed the beer vendor, and after quickly downing another, he felt lightheaded and giddy in the warm January sun. He became mesmerized by the ball's flight, the tight spirals that seemed to float in the air like those mascots. He half-expected the balls to lift and lift and lift right up and out of the stadium.

Late in the second quarter, the Tigers mounted a long drive to the Longhorns' five-yard line. It was only third down, but they'd already wasted their timeouts. The threat of a score brought Neil into focus. The chanting intensified. The LSU and Texas bands belted out dueling songs. One of the LSU quarterbacks, Lynn Amedee, ran onto the field with time ticking down. The ball was snapped, Amedee stepped forward, and Neil heard the thump of his foot on the ball and then watched it fly like a big brown bird through the goalposts. The scoreboard read eight seconds.

"Let's go up there," Neil said, pointing behind him to the stadium's lip. "I want to see what it's like at the top."

They wormed through the crowd, past the concession stands and bathrooms, and then through the shaded cement underworld of the stadium, into the tunnels to the upper section. They came out of the tunnel and then climbed another hundred steps to the last row.

"You can get a nosebleed up here," Ben said.

"Where are Uncle Jimmy's binoculars?" Neil asked.

"I thought you had them."

"Crap!"

The LSU band spread across the field like a blanket. The sun glinted off the horns. Neil could not make out any individual, just the swirled blue and yellow patterns plotted out so rigorously by the band for just this moment.

"Look this way," Ben said, his elbows propped on the back wall of the stadium. Neil turned and gazed at the Dallas skyline, the silver-glassed skyscrapers shimmering. He watched the puffy contrail in the wake of a plane and searched the sky for those balloon-flying mascots. Were they hovering somewhere, waiting to float back down into the stadium? He wished they hadn't left the binoculars in the truck. He looked down at the treetops and the sidewalk and the canopied vendors outside the stadium, saw a few people moving like insects. He had the urge, a residue from the two beers, to climb up on the ledge and just leap.

"We better head back down," Ben said. "The second half's about to start."

Neil wanted to stand up here for a while, see the game from this perspective. "Go ahead. I'll be along in a minute."

"You sure?"

Neil nodded and then watched Ben walk back down the steps, his thin figure growing thinner before he disappeared. A few minutes later, the teams returned to the field. The Tigers kicked off. A Longhorn caught it and started up the field. The runner looked like he might break free. Neil could see the gap where he should go; it was so clear from this view. But then several Tigers converged on the runner at once, and the ball squirted loose. Neil assumed it was beneath the heaving pile of jerseys and helmets around the thirty-five yard line. The refs untangled the mass, and at the end a Tiger jumped up and ran around triumphantly.

A few plays later, the Tiger quarterback scampered in for a twenty-two yard touchdown. 10-0. The Longhorns were doomed, Neil was sure, but he no longer really cared. It was the wonder of being in this stadium on this New Year's Day that he knew he would remember.

He didn't make his way back to his seat until the fourth quarter.

"What happened to you?" Ben asked, perturbed.

"Got lost," Neil said, smiling, holding out another beer to his brother.

They drank and cheered through the anticlimactic finish. Texas never recovered. They bobbled the ball the rest of the game, turning it over five times, and LSU added another field goal late in the fourth quarter. The Longhorns ended the day humiliated, their great season ruined by a shameful 13-0 shutout.

Neil and Ben spilled into the parking lot with what seemed a million other people. Neil felt again the enormity and absurdity of this event, how exotic to file into this concrete dish with so many other people to watch fifty boys chase a pigskin around for nearly three hours. He and Ben agreed that they were fortunate to live in America rather than some god-awful place like Africa or Russia where they couldn't stop starving or standing in line for a loaf of stale bread long enough to give a damn about something as magnificently frivolous as the 1963 Cotton Bowl.

After the game, they wandered the streets of downtown Dallas, ambling drunkenly from bar to bar. Unlike the Irish woman, the bartenders didn't seem to care that Ben was only seventeen. The glasses, Neil figured. Everyone thought you were older if you wore glasses. Besides, Ben charmed them all. If you acted like you belonged, no one questioned you, unless they happened to have a special arrangement with the police chief that threatened their livelihood. Of course, the bars were so packed with post-game partiers, many of them not much older than Ben, that the bartenders had no time to be discerning about the liquor laws. Neil and Ben moved from table to table and argued the finer points of the game. Neil nearly got punched by an LSU fan when he said that the Tigers were just a bunch of inbred Cajuns, but Ben soothed things over by ordering a couple of pitchers of beer for the table, and they wound up sitting with that group of Tigers and their girlfriends for two hours, until by the end they agreed that Okies and Cajuns were certainly the best damn breed of men and women on God's favorite continent, as well as the rightful descendents of a secret nobility. They all toasted and then belched their approval, and when they parted, they bear-hugged and grunted, and the LSU fan who'd nearly decked Neil told him there were no hard feelings. To prove it, he offered up his girlfriend, a chubby giggling brunette, for a smooch. Neil took her in his arms and gave her a sloppy, tongue-entwined kiss as everyone chanted, "Hook 'em, Horns! Hook 'em, Horns! Hook 'em, Horns!"

Their spirits buoyed, Neil and Ben left, searching for a late-night burger joint but finding instead a thin, ragged little shop with a purple sign dangling from the awning that said "Madame Tsontakis—Discover Your Future." A yellow light brightened the awning, and the sign on the door said, "Open for Prophecy."

Ben pointed to the small placard in the window that claimed "Only $2 for the Future!" He laughed. "What d'ya say?"

The smoky parlor had black wood paneling and dark antique tables with gold velvet tablecloths. Lamps covered in red-tasseled satin made the room burn. A Greek Orthodox Bible was displayed on a wooden bookstand. Though the room was cramped, it smelled rich and sweet. What was the name of that pastry Neil had tasted and loved so much during the trip to Washington, D. C.? The crust sticky and flaky, the filling made of meat-textured sweets, the only time he'd ever thought of those words together: *sweet* and *meat*.

Madame Tsontakis. What a complicated sight she was. Frizzy hair the color of red pepper; a black shawl with lace trim wrapped around her shoulders; a thick, floor-length maroon satin dress. Her face was a peculiar mixture of youth and old age. She didn't have a wrinkle on her, but her skin was slightly mottled on her cheeks and around her lips. Her nose was thin and aristocratic, her eyes bulbous and sensuously green and asymmetrical—as if pieces of beautiful shale were lodged in her irises. She could have been thirty-five or sixty, and she carried herself with the grace and feline warmth of a woman who'd had many lovers. Neil was immediately attracted to her. She took his hand in hers, which were surprisingly soft, and caressed it as if she were already foretelling his future. *Baklava!* Madame Tsontakis' hands carried the name of that Greek pastry.

"Come, sit down, the both of you," she said in a thick, regal accent that echoed musically in the room. She gestured toward two high-backed upholstered chairs, brocaded with red and emerald stitching. After they were seated, she said, "Who will be first to know his future?"

Ben and Neil looked at each other across the red gloom and shrugged their shoulders.

"I warn you. I do not lie. If you do not wish to know your destiny, you should leave now. I will not be offended."

Ben snickered. "Do you vish to know de future?"

Madame Tsontakis clutched Ben's hand and pressed her face close to his and said sharply, "You, little joker. You will be first. Come with me."

She led him through beaded curtains into another room, where Neil could see them on either side of a small table, sheathed with a cloth the shade and texture of Madame Tsontakis' shawl. She held both his hands and made him take off his glasses, and then she ran her fingers over his face slowly, across his forehead, eyes, and lips. She sat down and held his hands and spoke intently to him. Neil could not make out what she was saying but could hear the low, musical thrum of her voice. After a few minutes, Ben slipped through the beads and sat down silently. He looked shaken.

"How was it?" Neil asked.

Madame Tsontakis said, "See for yourself."

She held out her hand to Neil. He took it and again felt an erotic charge, this time mixed with dread. He passed through the beads and sat at the table. Madame Tsontakis demanded that he roll up his sleeves and lay his hands flat. She closed her eyes and ran her fingers over the backs of his wrists and then traced her fingernails sharply over his forearms to the crook of his elbow. She stood up, circled behind him, touched his shoulders, and then placed her fingers on his neck and under his collarbone in a way that made him dizzy. He didn't move. She ran her fingers over his thinly fuzzed jaw, and then circled in front of him and put her face so close to his that he could smell her breath, the faint aroma of something sweet, a Greek liqueur perhaps—or could it be baklava? She put her lips to his eyes. Her breath parted his lashes. Then she kissed him lightly on each eyelid.

"You will soon leave your home," she said, sitting down across from him. She clutched both of his hands. "You will fall in love. But love will not stay rooted in your heart. You will yearn to own a piece of the world. You will fall from the sky.

Your friends will die. You will dream of death. Insects will devour you, but you will rise from this feast. You will own the West. You are born for greatness. Your ambition, however, will overreach your humility. Then you will die."

"What do you mean?" he asked, feeling drugged.

She leaned back, smiled, and said, "You have heard what I mean."

"That's all?"

"'*That's all?*' I have warned you of your greatness. Take heed. Four dollars—for you and your friend."

"He's my brother."

"Your brother cannot be your friend?"

The drugged feeling left him. He was suddenly alert and embarrassed, and felt as if he'd been cheated and then called a fool. He paid her, and he and Ben left without saying a word.

They ate a late-night breakfast in silence at a truck stop down the street and looked out the greasy window at the neon glow of the parking lot. Neil finally asked Ben what Madame Tsontakis had told him. Ben fidgeted nervously and then said, "That I will love and kill many men."

"What does that mean?"

"Hell if I know," Ben said, shrugging his shoulders and looking down into the congealed remains of his gravy and biscuits. "What'd she tell you?"

Neil hesitated. He figured that she'd told Ben more than he had revealed, and Neil wondered if he should make a joke of it. "I'm destined for greatness," he finally said. "I'll fall out of the sky. Insects will eat me."

Ben laughed. "You fall out of the barn every week, and the mosquitoes and chiggers eat us both. That's no future. That's your *life*, man."

Neil laughed, too, but neither of them could entirely dismiss what had happened, nor did they know how to talk about it. Neil thought about their mother, who would also make pronouncements about the future and could sometimes mysteriously tell them what cards they held in their hands when they played Rook or Spades, but she would not approve of their visit to a fortuneteller, even if Madame Tsontakis did have a Bible in the room.

They rolled and lit cigarettes, rehashed the sad injustice of the Cotton Bowl, and pretended that Madame Tsontakis and her two-dollar fortunes were not that important. She didn't even know how to read palms or tarot cards or bones you shake in a magic dish and throw on the table. They went to the truck and climbed into the back. The night was warmer than the last, but still chilly. Neil asked Ben if he wanted to sleep in the cab.

"Naw," Ben said.

They pulled the scratchy horse blankets over them. Neil lay awake for a long time, hovering between consciousness and sleep.

"You may be destined for greatness," Ben said just as Neil was nodding off. "But I'll always have a bigger dick than you."

Ben perfectly caught Uncle Jimmy's voice and delivery. You had to love Ben. Even though he was too damn skinny and goofy-looking in his glasses with that smattering of freckles, he'd still been able to win over the whores and bartenders and Cajuns.

Above them, white-blue smoke gauzed the sky. In the distance, a train clickety-clacked over the rails. The air smelled faintly of manure. Neil thought about Madame Tsontakis' prophesy of greatness. Was the woman just full of two-dollar horseshit? What did it mean to fall from the sky? Kennedy nearly blew everybody sky-high last fall in his pissing contest with the Russians over the missiles in Cuba. The man was too young to be president, Harvey Lee argued, would probably wind up getting them all incinerated or send every man under twenty-five into Russia to storm the Kremlin. Uncle Jimmy had been a paratrooper. Maybe that's what lay in store for Neil. He'd parachute into Moscow, falling with a hundred thousand other idiots into a stadium filled to the brim with vodka.

And why would love not stay rooted in his heart? And how would insects devour him? And from what feast would he rise?

The woman was a loon, probably made the fortunes up in advance, crazy crap to spook or intrigue or flatter her customers, and vague enough so that anything she said could be later construed as truth. She was shrewd, though, you had to give her that, and there was something sexy about her, too, that voice and her talk and her fingers on his face and arms, and her beautiful, bulbous eyes, all of it an act to seduce you if you were fool enough, or to make you laugh, as if you were privy to a private joke, which—now that Neil thought about it—for two dollars wasn't a bad investment. Hell, he'd spent thirty dollars of Uncle Jimmy's money on a couple of five-minute joyrides, not counting the freebie that Gillian had given him. What was two bucks per fortune? Did Madame Tsontakis believe what she said? Did she indeed have a gift? Who knew? It didn't really matter. That was the way to sell yourself to the world—with a half-mad sense of belief in your own powers of prophecy and a withering matter-of-fact disdain for those who failed to appreciate your gifts. He'd have to remember that.

The white-blue smoke moved past. Maybe it wasn't smoke after all, just clouds obscuring the stars, but the sky was clear now, and bright and very still with a three-quarter moon frozen like an ice cube in the night. He examined the sky, imagined falling from the moon, floating through all that cold, black space—like John Glenn, orbiting Earth last February like a canned monkey. But what a lovely sight, and what a tremendous feeling coming back through the atmosphere, burning, burning, and praying that the parachutes held as you swayed in your toy capsule to the pillowy ocean. He'd watched Glenn on a little black-and-white TV at the VFW in Mangum with everyone else in the county, watched on the fuzzy screen as this beautiful, smiling American man fell from the sky, a modern miracle—ambition triumphing over humility.

II

Wedding Photograph, June 1963

There are no photographs of my mother as a child. I have, however, boxes of snapshots she's taken. She even engaged in a fanatical experiment when I was two, photographing me every day for an entire year to chart my incremental growth. It wasn't that her family was excessively poor, though they were poor, or that they had a religious opposition to cameras. Perhaps because my mother's older sister and my grandmother were both gone from the family before my mother turned fifteen, there was no official historian.

This explains, in part, why my mother became so compulsive about taking pictures once she married and had her own children, as if she tried to visually record the history of her present life since the visual history of her past was an enormous absence, blurred images that floated around the edges of her memories and dreams. It is ironic, too, since she has, for all her efforts to record her life, performed something of a disappearing act herself. I have not heard from her in more than four years. It's been much longer since I've seen her.

This photograph is the earliest one, when she was nineteen. From this wedding picture, I can imagine the eight, eleven, fifteen-year-old girl who was my mother. Both the girl and the woman reside together in the same body. She has her hair bouffanted in the frizz-and-spray technique that left adolescents from that era looking thirty. In the modest chiffon of her dress, her breasts are full. Her body possesses the voluptuousness of an older woman's.

Her abdomen, in the sheen of the studio light, slightly swells.

But her cheeks still have their baby plumpness, which will be gone in just a few years, and there is, too, a girlish pucker to her lips. In her eyes, you can see, beyond the posed formality, the mixture of stubbornness, curiosity, obedience, and confused apprehension that must have been the conflicting conditions of her adolescence. Also there is, unmistakably (at least for me), the delight of the young, the naïve surety that she has turned a corner, that she's in control of her destiny, that the shadow of her childhood will not follow her, that happiness awaits.

Perhaps I have brooded over this photograph too long, but I think I can see, even in the sepia tint, the thrumming, silky flush of a young bride, a heat and vulnerability emanating from the girl still in the process of becoming a woman, a butterfly emerging from a chrysalis. Beautiful, wetly radiant in the sunlight. Yet also easy prey.

In the dark chambers of her body, like a secret, I am forming.

Blind

A sun lamp, a sleeping pill, my mother dozing without the UV peepers over her eyes. Dark, troubled, shake-of-the-head talk from my father on the phone with the doctor. Mother in her bright blue terrycloth robe, her face burned blood red and blistered, her eyes blistered too, the wreckage hidden beneath the cotton bandaged to her sockets, helped up the stairs by my father. *This hand on the railing, now step up. Now that hand, that's right, easy does it.* An anxious servility in him.

The experience two decades later of seeing, for the first time, *Oedipus Rex*, that subversive song of pride and shame. The blind prophet Tiresias pointing his gnarled finger at Oedipus, exclaiming in John Gielgud's majestic warble: *You, you are the unclean thing. You are the one who must go.*

But back then, in Dallas, at the Old Mill Stream Apartments, I thought only of myself. Did I worry about my mother? Yes, certainly yes. But folding the *Times Herald* in the dark, four in the morning, beneath the apartment stairs, alone, I imagined what it would be like to have a blind mother. I could see it, a life marked out as significant, a source of pity and fear. The world of Braille, wooden canes, hairy shepherds: that's what I wanted, what I shamefully longed for.

Even then I yearned for tragedy, could taste the aesthetics of suffering.

Oh, how strange and tender are the dark fantasies of children. I was disappointed in a way I'd never articulate, even to myself, when the bandages were unspun from her eyes, her vision miraculously restored, like a gift from the gods.

No excuses now, no spectacular catastrophe, no special privilege or catharsis for her pitiable son, *The Child of the Blind Woman*. Just more papers to fold and rubber band in the dark, without her help. Then out on the roads by sunrise, pushing my grocery cart full of news, not a boy in exile, but merely a messenger, the black print all over my hands and face and coat, so that when I returned home, to where my parents slept, humbled and relieved, between newly washed sheets, I was only too aware that I was the dirty one. I was the unclean thing.

CHALKDUST ON A DRESS

> ...*it is ridiculous*
> *for streaks of chalkdust on a dress*
> *to assume the resonance*
>
> *of brushstrokes in Renoir.*
> *But that is how love goes...*
>
> —Tony Hoagland, "A Love of Learning"

Strange, how chalkdust on a dress can assume such resonance. It never makes much sense. The crosshatched white powder, like a sugared donut, on the blue cotton and polyester blend makes you see her for the lovely creature she is. Lovely, lovely Miss Downy, who plays Simon and Garfunkel on the portable record player she brings to class, who helps you appreciate the poetry of "I Am a Rock." Oh, how she glows in the light of the overhead transparency, *a rock feels no pain* in blurry fat lines across the raised ruffles of her chest, the black silk of her hair knotted in a honeybun with two red Japanese chopsticks. And in the back row, you cross your legs, mesmerized by chalk, transformed by her nyloned kneecaps and calves and shins and sandaled toes: so elegantly formed, as thin and beautiful as your hockey stick.

And then it happens. She asks you to stay late. After the buses leave, you beat the erasers on the sidewalk. The white powder rises from the cement and surrounds you like a beautiful evaporated milk cloud. When you return, the eraser box carried as delicately as a treasured gift, there she is, bent over, the chopsticks on her desk, her silky hair like a black waterfall in front of her face. Oh, how you stare at the exposed nape of her neck, that delicious white curve like the chicken breasts your mother cooked last night. She strokes her hair with a bone-handled brush you wish you had given her, the bristles working thickly, kissing and straightening. All you can do is stand there with that box of erasers and gape.

"Oh, Miss Downy, I love you!" you want to shout, but your tongue clings to the roof of your mouth. She twists her hair and stabs the chopsticks through. She runs a hand across the pleats of her chalk-streaked dress. When finally she sees you, a smile crosses her lips.

"Put it down over there, sweetie," she says. Two quick steps later, she bends before you and wipes chalkdust from the spray of freckles across your nose and cheeks. She leans in so close you can smell the peppermint of her breath. "Can you keep a secret?" she asks.

"Yes," you say, your eyes buggy.

"I'm getting married."

Your heart clangs against its cage. You want to say, *No! That chalkdust is mine!*

But she drapes her delicate, fingernail-painted hand on your shoulder and, still smiling, says, "Next month, you can call me Mrs. Subotnick."

She kisses your forehead and then turns away from you.

Walking home, the gasoline from the freeway hot and nauseous in your nostrils, you try your best to imagine it: chalkdust on the dress of Mrs. Subotnick. But the magic doesn't work. The poetry's all gone.

And that is how love goes.

Bad Weather

It was the night before your wedding, and you—a red-headed, gangly seventeen-year-old kid who still walked on tiptoes—drove my father's new Cadillac Eldorado. Nobody wore seatbelts then, at least not in West Texas where there was too much open space to hurt anything, including yourself. Rain poured, suddenly, in pelting sheets, and you turned, nervous, jumpy, your knuckles white on the steering wheel. In the distance lightning crinkled the black, enormous sky. I wasn't worried. I trusted you, my uncle, as I trusted all adults then. I nodded in the seat beside you, my head bobbing up and down in loose-necked drowsiness, the rain thumping an insistent rhythm on the hood and roof and windows, like a pulse, like a lullaby, the Cadillac's wipers a quiet *whish-whoosh*, slapping away the watery blindness.

Then the sound of brakes squealing in water, a thrusting forward and a tap on my forehead.

I turned to you, as you hunched over the steering wheel, and smiled. I followed your stricken eyes to the windshield where we watched the spider web creep across the rain-spattered glass. It seemed then like a remarkable thing. I wondered what had happened. Had we hit some animal? Did a truck shoot gravel?

"Are you okay?" you asked, and I laughed.

You touched my face, yet I couldn't feel your fingers on my skin. The passenger-side mirror revealed a shiny bulb blooming on my forehead. That, too, seemed remarkable, as if my head and my *self* were two different things. I laughed again. But you started to cry because it was the day before your wedding to your first wife, a girl no older than yourself. Your sister and her husband had entrusted you with their son and overpriced car, and you would now be driving up to the church, late for the rehearsal dinner, a cracked windshield, your nephew with a lump on his forehead the size of Amarillo—death inevitable—and it could only be your own damn fault.

The look on your face: *Oh God, what have I done?* Your eyes round and green like marbles, your nostrils flared, betrayal written on your face.

What I want to tell you now is that I was the one who betrayed you. I was fine, the accident a wonderful *event*, an exciting kiss of disaster, all the more exhilarating because I escaped unharmed except for the knot on my forehead, which didn't hurt, didn't even scar me, but allowed me to upstage you, to bathe in the family's sympathy, a pampering of cloth-wrapped ice cubes, and all the Coke, cookies, cake, and peppermints I could eat while you tried to explain your sorry-ass self. It made the trip memorable, though it poisoned your wedding, tainted it in the spooky way bad weather and accidents will do.

Over the years, I betrayed you in other ways, too, ways you would never know. When I was thirteen and came to stay with your pretty, dark-haired wife, to help her pack while you went rigging off-shore, I listened from my bedroom as you made love to her the night before you left. While you were gone I tried to kiss her, plotted ways that week to look down her blouse, to spy her emerging naked from the shower or with only a towel wrapped loosely around her wet breasts.

Later, when I was sixteen, I kissed and then made love to one of your lovers, a girl you had even proposed to, but she wouldn't marry you, said you were trouble. She seduced me because I was your nephew, which I knew had its advantages. As my lips and fingers brushed her flesh, I felt sorry for you, though not sorry enough to stop.

The year before you died, I wrote a story about you. You were a railroad worker; you beat your estranged wife, though you loved her. On the night I depicted in the story, you saw her in a bar, argued with her, drove her into a lake and nearly drowned yourself and everybody else, and when your wife started to tell you she did not love you anymore, you swam down into your sunken Nova and imagined yourself breathing the murky water. Your lungs exploding, you swam at the last second for the night air, and when you wiped the water from your burning eyes and caught your breath, you sought the shore and then the water, but she was gone, and you were left hoping she would resurface.

So imagine my surprise when I got the call a few years later. There you are, in the shadow of my imaginary scenario, stalking your second ex-wife, following her from a bar where she would not talk to you, following her home in your truck to discover the police there. They know you only too well. They know you are not to be trusted, that you are a clumsy and dangerous man who carries bad weather in his heart. You park the truck, draw your revolver from the glove box, place the muzzle first against your barely-wrinkled forehead, but then, because you are sentimental man, center it over your heart. In the night, which is clear and moonlit but with the sweet smell of rain coming on, you gaze one last time at your home, splashed in the blue and red police lights, a double-wide trailer where your second wife and her son, who fears you as much as she does, stare at you from the window. The police, leaning against their cruisers, flashlights in hand, wait for your next move.

With the night as clear and calm and empty of confusion as you wish yourself to be, you squeeze the trigger, and what seems like lightning flashes in the truck.

I wonder what you felt in that instant—a half-dreamy happiness or loss, maybe only a slight tap on your chest. Was the pressure as light as the tap I felt on my head so long ago? I imagine it to be that soft.

Did you know you would leave all of us—the police, your ex-wives, your brothers, sisters, parents, your little girl, your stepson, your nephew—with the same wide-eyed, nostril-flared, *Oh shit, what could I have done to prevent this?* dread you felt as you looked at that five-year-old boy who was me and saw his head erupting before you, and watched the window cracking, which seems now, in my memory, not like a spider web at all but like the drowsy spider itself, waking and covering the entire windshield?

As I think about that rainy night more than thirty years ago, I remember, too, your laughter, your temporary relief when you discovered I was, except for the bump on my head, all right. I remember the thrill of helping you navigate through the rain, unable to see through that cracked windshield. I remember how you drove so slowly the rest of the way, with your head sticking out the side window of my father's Cadillac, trying to stay on the blacktop as the lightning flashed like a premonition in the distance and the rain exploded against your face.

Snipe Hunt

Not long after my parents divorced for the second and final time, my mother married Kent, a hydraulic tools salesman. He was short and muscled, only twenty-six—seven years her junior—with red hair, freckles, and a thick handsome mustache that twitched when he laughed. They went to Acapulco for their honeymoon, quarreled, and one night he shoved her out of a taxi and made her walk back to the hotel. But when they returned home to Houston, loaded down with sombreros, ironwood carvings of dolphins and turtles, and several bottles of tequila, they were smiling.

Later that fall, Kent took me, my mother, and my sister to his boss' home in the Piney Woods, about three hours from Houston. His boss, George, owned several hundred acres in the woods, a large main house, and a two-bedroom guest house, where our family stayed. The second night, my mother and sister and George's wife went to bed early, and I stayed up with Kent and George. George was a tall, stout man who wore square, black-rimmed glasses, long-sleeved flannel shirts, laughed heartily, and regarded Kent as his protégé.

It was cool in the evening, then cold and shadowy with the tall pines looming ominously around us. We sat on the picnic tables, the two men drinking from a bottle of Wild Turkey, encouraging me to partake, though I was not quite fourteen, which made me feel significant and included, even when they laughed as I sputtered and coughed after the first toxic gulp.

As they drank into the night, their stories grew elaborate, tales of the silver wolves of this region, how they ran in packs and how you could hear them howling at night, thrashing through the woods, sometimes even see, if you were lucky and not too drunk, the moonlight shining along the bristly hairs of their ears and backs. George talked at length about a neighbor of his who had been attacked by a wolf and barely survived. Then they started telling jokes and hunting stories, and finally they got around to stories about the snipe, whose pelt was worth a fortune, and whose meat was better than filet mignon, tender and delicious. George said snipe were all over his woods. He'd seen them earlier in the day, in fact, as Kent had been teaching me to shoot a rifle. He said they were easy to catch at night—dumb, small, harmless animals. All you had to do was jacklight them, that is, drive around with the truck until you found their warren, flip on your headlights, which would stun them, and chase them into a gunnysack someone held. Easy as pie. He'd done it a million times.

Within minutes, it was decided that we would catch us some snipe for George's wife to cook the next day. I was designated as the gunnysack holder. They drove me into the middle of the woods, gave me a flashlight.

"Now when you see it coming, point the flashlight in its eyes, and it'll run right for the sack," Kent said, draping his arm around my shoulder, smiling in a pleasant, fatherly way. "You got that?"

"I think so."

It was cold by now, air misting in front of our faces, and I had on Kent's coat, the sack in one hand, the flashlight in the other. George and Kent walked down the path to the truck and pulled away, crunching brush and rocks as they left. It was pitch black with the trees high around me. I could make out the moon, a half-crescent threaded through the branches of the pines. The truck raced around the woods, close by, then farther away, then after a few minutes I couldn't hear anything at all.

I stayed that way in the small clearing for what seemed an eternity, as the night grew quieter, more ominous. In the distance, in the direction of the main house, a howl, then another. George's bloodhound and German shepherd? A few minutes later, from a different direction, nearer, I heard another one. Over the next fifteen minutes, the howls kept getting closer, answering each other. I wanted to call out for Kent and George, but if they were gone, I didn't want to attract any attention. More time passed, but still nothing. I stood there still and stupidly with my gunnysack and flashlight, wishing they would show up, willing them to come back. What had happened to them? Where the hell were they?

At the time, I was going through my Edgar Rice Burroughs and Jack London phase. *Tarzan, The Return of Tarzan, The Son of Tarzan, Tarzan and the Forgotten City,*

Tarzan and the Jewels of Opar, The Call of the Wild, White Fang. Animals routinely shredded human flesh; apes tore the arms off natives, and packs of rabid wolves devoured human legs, faces, tore jugular veins.

The woods grew increasingly quiet. Too quiet. I heard an owl hoot, which startled me. Then another howl not far away, then another, then quiet, then a few minutes later, rustling in the trees, a low throaty growl.

"Kent?" I whispered. "George? Is that you?" Another rustle. Another growl. I froze, trying to control my breathing but was unable to. The crisp fall air scratched my throat. "Kent," I panted. I dropped the gunnysack, put the flashlight quickly in my coat pocket, the light still on and shining into my face.

A real growl now.

I shot toward the nearest tree, a tall thin one I knew I could get my arms around. Ten feet up were the first limbs. I shinnied up it as fast as I could, my breath raspy, thunderous in my head. The flashlight in my coat pocket flickered wildly in the tree above and on my face, blinding me.

Up as far as I could go, not quite to the first limb, I held on tight to the bark, heard more growls, the bushes rustling. I could picture it all too clearly now—the wolves jumping, snapping at my feet, waiting for me to tire, to fall asleep, slip down so they could tear into me. I'd read about it. I knew it could happen. And what about that neighbor of George's? It already *had* happened. *Please, God, please, please, please.* Scare them off, that's what I'd do. I would scream or sound furious, and if they jumped up or climbed the tree, I would bang them on their snouts with the flashlight. I could feel shit seeping into my underwear.

"Kent! George!" I screamed. "Somebody help me!"

Tears streamed down my face. *Oh, God, please, I don't want to die! Don't let me die, don't let me die, don't let me die. Please God, please God, please God.*

Then I heard it.

I didn't know what it was at first. But then I heard it again—a different kind of howl from the bushes. I grabbed the flashlight with my hand, bloody from scraping it on the bark of the tree, and shone the light below. On the carpet of the clearing where I'd been, I could make out two figures, lying down, their legs in the air, holding their stomachs, unable to speak, to even breathe.

"Kent?" I called meekly from the tree. "George?" Had they been attacked? Tried to save me and now were dying below me?

Then a wave of noise ripped from their throats, and I recognized it for what it was.

"Oh, Jesus!" they yelped, "SOMEBODY HELP ME!"

"Oh, please God, please God, don't let them eat me."

"Don't let me die, don't let me die, don't let me DIE!"

Then they were on their backs again, rolling around in a fit of convulsive laughter. I was speechless.

After he got control of himself, Kent yelled, "Come on down, Tarzan."

I slid down the tree, carefully, my fingers and palms raw and wet with blood, the flashlight flickering over my face again, spotlighting my humiliation.

Kent ambled over, wrapped one arm around my shoulder, and wiped the tears from his face with his other hand. I could smell the Wild Turkey on his breath. He started to say something, then broke into giggles again and had to bend over and place both hands on his knees to steady himself.

George said, "Good snipe hunting, boy!"

"Jesus, you should have seen yourself up there," Kent said, his teeth white in the moonlight, his face glistening with tears, his red mustache twitching. "That flashlight jerked around like two grasshoppers fucking."

And they both were on the ground yet again while I stood there dumbly. Finally, they were able to collect themselves. George tousled my hair and led us toward the truck.

"What's that smell?" he said, as we walked down the path.

"Smells like Tarzan stinkied his loincloth," Kent said.

After a month or two, my mother and Kent started going out to bars to shoot pool with friends and would come home late, sometimes just my mother first, storming in, making a beeline for the bedroom, her wig a little crooked on her head, the mascara creating a teary raccoon mask around her eyes. She would lock herself in. A few minutes later, Kent would knock on the front door. He'd inevitably lost his keys, or couldn't find them in the dark, and would be calling my mother's name: "Open up, honey pie." When she would ignore his pleas, he would beat on the door, hammering the knocker until finally, out of embarrassment, I went to it.

I have a thick, vivid image of him, seen through a peephole, his shirt unbuttoned at the collar and untucked from his slacks, his tie loosened and flipped over his shoulder like a noose, his red hair shooting in various directions, two points, like horns, above his ears. He smiles thinly, one of his brows arched in a drunken attempt at irony, that mustache twitching. He puts his eyeball to the other side of the peephole, stares through, laughs like we're old buddies.

"Hey, Tarzan," he whispers, "let me in."

I remember that fall, winter, and spring as a time of unlocking and locking doors, peering through peepholes, gauging the danger level, waiting for the wolf to blow the house down.

I would let him in during those early days, and he would talk, nonsensically, an edgy giggle in his voice, his monologue full of non-sequiturs. He'd ask me how my day was. Any calls for him? Was I getting any pussy yet? At least playing kissy-face? God, how old was I? Fourteen? Too old to be a virgin. Did I know he won eight pool games straight, ran the table on one, kissed some cunt in a purple mini-skirt, which made my mother mad as hell? Hahahahaha.

He'd unloosen the tie slowly during this monologue, fold it neatly, set it on the couch. He'd take off his belt, loop it around my shoulders. On and on he'd go, jabbering away, wherever his mind would take him, as he slowly undressed, seemingly uninterested in my mother's whereabouts, totally focused on me. Off would come his shirt, which he'd drape over a nearby chair, and he'd rub his chest and stomach, thick and impressively matted with reddish brown hair, and lie down, finally, on the couch, a pillow propped under his head, still talking away, smoothly, clearly. A salesman.

"Oh, Tarzan, you should have seen me. Five ball, corner pocket. Bam. Three ball, side pocket. Whop. Triple bank shot for the four. The eight ball behind the back, an easy, slow glide, a gentle nudge, and the flow over felt to the pocket. She was just there, a secretary, for chrissakes, just a little celebratory kiss. That's all it was. Just a little thank you, Kent-a-roni, for the show."

And then he'd be asleep, and I'd drape an afghan over him, turn out the lights, and head back to bed.

"Where is he?" my sister would whisper from her bed.

"Asleep."

"Are you sure?"

"It's okay. Go to sleep."

My mother's door never opened.

Other times, late at night, after we'd gone to bed, I'd hear them in their bedroom, things being knocked off dressers, my mother saying, "Kent, don't, that hurts. Quit it, you're hurting me." Sometimes there would be little gasps or crying. My room was next to theirs, and I would try to make out what was going on in there. Was he hurting her? I would think so, and then there would be a silence, followed by the bedsprings squeaking and the headboard tapping the wall, and I would feel confused and angry and stupid. Then other times, I would hear shouting, a muted scream, things breaking, and I would race to their door, my ear against the wood, then hesitantly knock and ask, "Mom, is everything all right?"

After a too-long pause, during which I could hear fierce, incomprehensible whispering, my mother would call out in a false-calm voice, "I'm just fine, honey. Go on back to bed."

Sometimes Kent would appear at the door, his hair sticking up, rubbing his matted chest, smiling pleasantly. "Everything's fine. Don't you worry."

I'd look beyond him to my mother on the bed, in her nightgown, sitting Indian-style, angry sometimes, other times with her head in her hands. Once I remember her looking pitifully at me. She seemed to be telling me something with her eyes. *I'm in trouble,* they said. *Help me.* But Kent would smile, tug my arm, prod me gently, humorously into my own room.

"Tarzan got big test tomorrow. Tarzan needs his beauty sleep." He'd wink like we were conspirators, then shut his door and turn on the television in their room, so I couldn't hear anything.

The next day I would study my mother's face and arms for bruises, gauging her demeanor, searching for clues to this puzzle. I couldn't figure it out, though. Most mornings she was cheery, but other times she seemed hung-over, or pained, and on those mornings, she shut me out when I asked her what was the matter, or she would hug me close but not say a word, as if the hug was her way of expressing what she would not allow herself to tell me.

One morning, following an episode like this, she said divorcing my father was a mistake, the worst mistake she'd ever made in her life. She regretted it, but what was there for her to do now? She'd made her bed and now she had to lie in it.

This fatalistic attitude frightened me, made me sick and worried while I was at school, superstitious when coming home, sure that something terrible had happened or was going to happen soon, and that I was not going to be there to stop it. Or worse, that I was going to be there, but not be *able* to stop it. I dreaded the walk from the bus to the apartment. I'd stay at my friends' houses when I could. I tried to push it from my mind, but it would surface in my dreams, where Kent loomed above me with his bloodshot eyes, his hair in that familiar drunken tangle, smiling with a sliver of pink tongue between yellow teeth as he exploded buckshot into our bodies, smiling as he strangled us, smiling as he chopped up our bodies into a thousand little pieces.

I became quiet and sullen and wary in that apartment, trying to decode mysterious messages in the most innocuous of conversations. There was no one I dared share any of these thoughts with. I didn't want to be seen as a coward for not doing something to save my mother and sister.

. . .

Later that spring, I went out of town on a camping trip with a friend's family, and when I came back a week later, the front windows of our apartment were boarded up. I unlocked the door, but it wouldn't move. My mother lifted a piece of wood, released the deadbolt, and unleashed the security chain.

"What's going on?" I asked, and she informed me that Kent was gone, they were through, finished, kaput. The man was a lunatic, nuts. My mother had dark purplish bruises on her neck. Her left eye was puffy and swollen and a little yellowish on the brow.

I learned from her, and later from my sister, that while I was gone, Kent had gone berserk and twice tried to kill my mother. On one occasion, he put a revolver in her mouth and threatened to shoot. A few days later, my sister heard scuffling in the bathroom, and when she opened the door, she found my mother in the tub, her feet thrashing, Kent over her with his arms plunged into the water around her neck. My sister said the first thing she saw was our mother's face under the water, her eyes wide open, eyebrows arched in fear, bubbles streaming from her mouth. How my mother escaped, I have no idea. The police came but did essentially nothing except encourage her to file assault charges and get a restraining order, neither of which she did. But Kent reluctantly left. He threatened to be back, though.

"Just you wait," he'd said.

I yearned for ignorance. As it was, my mother and particularly my sister seemed to look to me for answers. I didn't have any. The stories confirmed my nightmares, so I shut them out, tried to convince myself they hadn't happened. I wanted to cop a feel of my girlfriend's breasts, play football and baseball and Monopoly with my friends, sneak into movies, and read more Edgar Rice Burroughs and Jack London novels—those narratives of escape and rescue, of attack and self-preservation. I didn't want to worry anymore about Kent and what he was going to do to us.

My father was somehow immune from all this. In fact, we were forbidden by my mother to tell him what had happened, which was easy enough for me to do. I didn't want to talk about it with anyone.

Besides, there were others to protect us. The police, supposedly. But there was also Bob, our family friend for many years. Bob was tall with a kid's face, chubby cheeks, a thin nose. He had black hair, a mustache, and a little potbelly. He was kind and funny, sort of a know-it-all, but you could forgive him that. The main thing was that we knew him; we trusted him. He felt like part of the family. He had in fact been my father's best friend, though they no longer spoke to each other.

One time, before Kent left, my mother took my sister and me with her to Bob's efficiency apartment, where they talked in hushed whispers in the kitchen while we watched cartoons. I remember them standing there, my mother with her eyes closed, tears running down her face, Bob holding her close, consoling her, stroking her back.

He gave me his number and told me to call him anytime I wanted, if I ever needed to talk about anything, or if I needed any help, or just wanted to play some rummy for a penny a point.

After Kent left, we saw a lot of Bob. It was his idea and handiwork to board up the windows. He would come over and spend evenings with us, and weekends we would go out with him to the beach or the movies or to restaurants. I slept better knowing he was around.

After a couple of months, Kent seemed resigned to the impending divorce and, from what we could tell from informants in his office, was somewhat penitent about his behavior. We took the boards off the windows and relied on the standard security locks. My nightmares stopped. We all felt more relaxed.

The last night I saw Kent seems surreal but yet, so many years later, all too vivid in my imagination, and always in the present tense.

It is night. My mother and sister and I are home, watching a movie in my mother's room and playing canasta. Bob is not there. And suddenly, with no warning, Kent stands before us in the doorway of the bedroom. Everything that follows seems to happen in slow motion, like we're swimming in molasses.

He wears light brown slacks, a plaid shirt, loafers. His hair is combed, but his eyes look a little red; I can't tell if he's drunk. I'm the first to see him. I jump, let out a gasp. Then my mother and sister, a split second later, simultaneously scream. Their faces, as I turn to them, are stricken, my mother's eyes comically bugged, her mouth open. My sister clutches my mother, buries her face in her arm and starts to whimper.

Kent leans against the doorjamb. He smiles, pleased by our response.

"I've missed you," he says calmly.

We do not know what he means by this, or why he is here, or how he got in, or what he plans to do. We do not move, do not utter a sound. Even my sister stops her whimpering but keeps her head down. I do not make direct eye contact with him, either. Kent stands there, waiting for us to move, waiting for us to speak, waiting patiently, leaning in the door, smiling.

My mother breaks the silence. "What do you want, Kent?" She says this so calmly, so smoothly, her voice low and firm, that I cannot help but admire her. She looks him straight in the eye, not defiantly, but not fearful either.

"My things," he says. He means, I believe, some clothes, a few knick-knacks, and his guns. He has a rifle and a revolver in the closet. My mother has kept them for protection, but now keeping them in the house seems like a stupid move.

"You're not supposed to be here," my mother says.

"This is my apartment. I pay the rent."

"You are not supposed to be here," she says again. Her voice is not threatening, nor angry. Steady and direct. She tells him, calmly, that she will gather the rest of his things if he will leave the apartment, and she will place them outside on the front porch, or, if it would be convenient, she will have them dropped off at his office.

He laughs—a short, derisive blast. Then, quickly, the maliciousness in that laugh is replaced with that pleasant, wicked smile.

"I want my things," he says, ignoring the options she has outlined.

My mother picks up the phone by her bed and begins to dial.

"What are you doing?" he says and moves around the bed toward the phone. My mother does not look at him, but she does not seem frightened either.

"My ex-husband has broken into my apartment," she begins, but before she can finish, his finger is on the clicker. He smiles at her. She reaches down and moves his finger from the clicker, which he allows her to do. Their actions are precise, controlled, almost formal. She begins to dial again, and while she is doing this, he takes hold of the clear plastic cord running from the phone to the wall and deftly snaps it from the outlet.

My sister covers her eyes with her hands and starts to cry. I, too, am startled by this but say nothing, looking to my mother for guidance. She stares at him for what seems an interminably long time, then turns and tells me to go to the other phone and call the police. I do not look at Kent, but walk briskly out of the room to the phone in the kitchen. Before I can dial, Kent is there, smiling that same smile he gave me through the peephole on those late nights when my mother would lock him out of the house. I can see, because of the fluorescent kitchen lights, Kent's face more clearly. He has been drinking, I can tell, but not so much that he can't be reasoned with.

Or so I think.

"Please leave, Kent." My voice is a plea. I want to appeal to him as my stepfather. "Don't do this."

"I'm just here to get my things," he says slowly, innocently, and the word *things* now means something else, something more abstract and insidious. He reaches across my face, takes the phone and puts it back on the hook, pops the cord from both the phone and the outlet, then loops the plastic cord around his hand.

He winks at me, and in that moment, in that wink, I am suddenly shaken with fear. I know now that my mother's and sister's stories were true. The man is capable of anything.

He turns and gets himself a glass from the cabinet. I bolt toward the bedroom, where my mother is in the closet, trying either to hide the guns or get them out, I can't tell which. My sister still cries. Whispering, I tell my mother he's popped the cord from the other phone, and she tells me to get out as fast as I can and call the police from the neighbor's. Tell them there are guns in the house. Hurry.

I don't want to go, but she presses, tells me I have to. I start for the door, but then Kent is there, in the doorway. My sister screams, and at the sight of him, I sprawl back on the bed. My mother is there with her arms around my sister. Kent stands with a glass of clear, iced liquid in one hand, the phone cord looped around his wrist. He bugs his eyes, arches his eyebrows, lolls his tongue in a parody of a lunatic.

"Oooohhh!" he says.

Then he starts to flick the light switch off and on, laughing.

"Quit it!" my mother yells, sharp and angry now, which makes him happy. This is what he has wanted all along and what my mother has not given him since that first frightened scream of hers: emotion. He keeps flicking the light off and on, faster now.

"Stop it!" my mother yells again. He twirls the phone cord in his hand, sips his drink. He flicks the light off, and then, for some reason I'll never know, he turns and walks back toward the kitchen.

My mother whispers, "Go!" I run for the front door and try to undo the deadbolt and the chain, but then I see Kent's shadow in the living room.

"What are you doing?" he shouts.

I run back to my bedroom, close the door, lock it. I raise my window, kick out the bug screen. We live on the second story of a two-story apartment building. Directly below me is thorny shrubbery, then a thin patch of grass, maybe three feet between the bushes and the sidewalk. I wear only a t-shirt and shorts. No shoes, no socks, but there is no time to waste. My legs and arms tingle. Bile rises in my throat, and when I swallow, it burns. The drop is maybe fifteen feet. I climb out the window, clutching the edge, then hold my breath, count one, two, and on three, I kick off the side of the building and fly through the dark night air.

My feet catch the sting, which travels through my ankles, past my knees and thighs into my groin. But I've landed where I wanted to land, on the grass, missing both the shrubbery and the sidewalk. I shake off the shock and then stumble across the courtyard to my friend Rudy Hernandez's apartment, and bang on the door until his father—a burly, strong-jawed man wearing only boxer shorts—answers. I tell him what has happened, urge him to do something and to please, please hurry.

Rudy stands behind him and hears everything. His father orders him to call the police and tells me to wait. He is back in a minute, shirt and pants on, and then we are out in the courtyard, along with the whole Hernandez family—Rudy, Emilio, Maria, and little Henry, Mrs. Hernandez in her floor-length nightgown, her thick black hair pinned in a net—all of us looking up into the window of my mother's room.

The light is on, but we can't see anything, not even shadows. I'm frightened and frantic and feel that this must be a mistake, my jumping out the window. I should be up there with them. He would not do anything with me there, or if he tried, I would at least be there to prevent it. I run for the balcony, which leads up to our back porch, which has a sliding glass door. I am on top of the downstairs wooden railing, my hands on the bottom slats of our balcony, when Mr. Hernandez pulls me down, tells me I have to stay here until the police come. He is right, I realize, and I am thankful that he has pulled me down, but in my heart I know I'm a coward, that I would rather let my mother and sister be hurt or even killed than have to suffer myself.

Mrs. Hernandez puts her hands on my shoulders, pats my head gently, and tells Mr. Hernandez to do something. They quarrel about this for a few seconds, then he asks me, "What is your stepfather's name?"

"Kent," I say.

"Kent what?"

"Kent McLure."

"Mr. McLure!" Mr. Hernandez calls. "Mr. McLure!"

No one answers, but the lights go off in the bedroom, and Mr. Hernandez is about to go to the front door when we see the police roll up, their flashers going, the red and blue lights whipping our windows. There are two policemen, and together they get information from me about the situation, then one of them climbs the stairs cautiously, his gun drawn, and hammers the clacker on the front door, while I wait at the bottom of the stairs with the other policeman.

"Mr. McLure," the policeman at the door says. "Mrs. McLure." He knocks again.

Moments later, I hear the deadbolt release, and Kent opens the door, the light from the hallway creating a halo around his tangled red hair. He is smiling, courteous, innocent. Everything is okay, everything's fine, he says. No need to worry.

My mother beckons them in, and the other policeman and I go upstairs and into the apartment, where I see my mother and sister in the living room, crying but apparently unharmed. Kent sits on the bed in my mother's room, talking politely to the first policeman, telling him that he just wanted his things, that's all. He is all smiles now, a portrait of sweetness, a salesman. I am ushered back into the living room, where I tell my version of the story, and then my mother and sister tell theirs. My mother wants him locked up, in jail, throw away the key. He could have killed us, she says. She is semi-hysterical, melodramatic. She possesses none of the poise she demonstrated earlier. I feel embarrassed for her, for us all.

The evening ends with the police telling us there is nothing they can do.

The apartment is registered in Kent's name, there is no restraining order, and despite the separation, he and my mother are still married, and in Texas there is little the police can do unless someone is injured or killed. They are sorry. They have talked Kent into leaving, however, and they have urged my mother to change the locks, to have someone we know stay at the apartment with us, and to file a restraining order.

From my window, I see the two policemen standing around Kent's car as he laughs. At one point, I hear the cops laugh, too, and I wonder if they are humoring him, or if they are really on his side, if they think my mother and sister and I are the stupid, hysterical ones.

I stay there at the window until Kent drives away, and then the Hernandez family files back into their apartment and turns off the lights. My mother has called Bob, and soon after he arrives, the police leave, and I stay up for a little while narrating the events of the night. We all go to bed, knowing Bob is there on our couch.

I lie beneath the covers with my eyes closed, trying to calm myself, but each time a car drives by, its lights strobing my window, my heart pumps harder. My leg shakes, spastically and inexplicably now, and I can feel the tingle again in my knees and ankles from the jump to the ground. I can't help but imagine how this night could have turned out, and the prospect of it, the scenario as it plays in my head, both frightens and thrills me.

But I sleep anyway, thankful that Bob, who will marry my mother in a few months, is snoring in the other room.

A Nova, a Secret, an Eyelash, a Snoring Man

1.

Between my freshman and sophomore years in high school, I moved from Houston to Amarillo, Texas, where I got a job, even though I was only fifteen, at a non-union movie theater. I was an usher, then concessionist, marquee changer, preview splicer, and ultimately a projectionist. Two other guys, Adam and Matt, worked there, both a year older than me. Adam was tall and thin, a baby-faced, sweet-tempered guy who was shy with girls. Matt was a flaxen-haired, flabby-bellied boy-man who liked to drink a lot of beer and tell dirty jokes. They took me under their wing, and we spent most of our time together, when we weren't at school or working at the theater, either driving around Amarillo in Adam's black Plymouth Barracuda or drinking beers at Matt's house with his identical twin, Mark.

Matt thought of himself as a lucky man. There was evidence for this. The next summer, on two consecutive nights, he found hundred-dollar bills on the floor of The Western Club. Emboldened by this luck, he put a down payment on a car, his first, a Chevy Nova. Adam and I were there with him and his father the afternoon he bought it. His father co-signed the loan, and that night we celebrated by getting a couple of six-packs and cruising around in the car. Matt drove to a medical district on the west side of town—a big place with a winding road and small lake in the middle of it. That was where other teenagers from the high school often congregated to make out, drink, or fight.

This particular night was hot and breezy. We had the windows down. I rode shotgun. Adam was in the backseat. Matt drove to the top of Medi-Park Drive, and then, wanting to see what his new car could do, he gunned it down the hill. He'd had a few too many beers, however, and when he hit a curvy patch of asphalt, wet from sprinklers, he touched the brakes, and we started to slide. He panicked and, rather than turn into the slide, he stomped on the accelerator, and soon we jumped the embankment. For a magically suspended moment—during which the three of us stared ahead with a kind of humorous, open-mouthed awe—we sailed through the air above the little Medi-Park lake. When we finally hit the water, we floated for a strange second or two. I distinctly remember Adam giggling in the backseat like a little kid. Then the front of the car dipped down and began sinking. Water flowed over the rolled-down windows into the seats. Matt tried to open the door, but it wouldn't budge, and he freaked out, shouting, "We're gonna drown, we're gonna drown!" He clambered out of his side window, tipping the car as it was sinking, and then I crawled out my side and fell into the water as the car was almost submerged. I didn't know what had happened to Adam. Had he been able to extricate himself from the backseat? I couldn't see him in the dark water. I struggled in my drenched clothes to find the surface. When I made it, gasping for air, I called out Adam's name but could hear and see nothing. I swam to shore, where Matt sat on the grass, rocking back and forth, as if keening, cursing at himself. Adam was behind him, water dripping from his clothes and hair.

 The strangest thing, out of all the strange things that happened that night, was that Adam was dancing back and forth on the balls of his feet, laughing. The sight of him there, so incongruous to the whole scene, as if he was still caught in the last stages of his giggling fit, made me laugh as well, even though I didn't want to. Matt's poor car was all but sunk, just the silver ball of the radio antenna glowing above the surface. It was clear that we'd survived something amazing, and the story, no matter how much trouble we got into, would be worth it. Adam just kept dancing and laughing.

 Later that summer, I met a girl and during the next year saw less and less of Adam and Matt. At the end of the school year, Adam left for the mountains of Colorado, either to go to college or to work, I can't remember. Matt had a job at an auto parts store, and I seldom saw him.

 Near the end of my senior year, I got a call from Matt. It was one of those calls that you know, even before you pick up the phone, will be bad news. He said that Adam had hanged himself. Adam's mother had contacted Matt and wanted the two of us to be pallbearers. She said that we were his best friends, which made me feel worse because I hadn't been in touch with him in over a year and didn't know what he had been doing in Colorado, what made him want to die. His funeral was closed-casket, so I never saw him again.

At the time that disappointed me.

At the gravesite, Matt, the other pallbearers, and I held up his coffin and turned in the direction of Adam's mother. She lifted her veil, and her face seemed literally cracked with grief. I had never seen, nor have I seen since, a face as ravaged by mourning as hers was. She was not old—perhaps late thirties or early forties at most—and I remembered, from my frequent visits to Adam's house, her being a good-looking woman. It shook me profoundly to see her face so transformed. I have never forgotten it.

After the funeral, Matt and I went out for a drink, and we resurrected our memories of Adam. The one that made us laugh and then quickly sobered us was the one of that night at Medi-Park, how we might have all drowned together, and how Adam had giggled through the whole disaster, as if privy to a joke we would never quite get.

2.

My family had moved to Amarillo when I was fifteen because my stepfather's secretary was murdered. My stepfather's name was Buz. He was my mother's fifth husband, and he had been the food service director for the University of Houston when my mother met him. That summer, after his secretary was killed, Buz and my mother married and decided, on a whim, to leave the mayhem of Houston, a redneck city that was also one of the murder capitals of the country.

I should describe the two of them in more detail to reveal some of the psychological valence of their marriage and help explain what happened later. At forty-four, he was ten years my mother's senior, but he looked older than that. He was skinny, maybe 140 pounds, though his arms had gone to middle-age flab. He was not that tall, yet looked even shorter because his posture was awful, his spine curving so that it appeared at times like he was a hunchback. He had thin, straw-like brown hair, going gray not only at the corners but, unbecomingly, on the top of his head. His face was long, tan, and creviced with curved wrinkles, like scythes, running from his nostrils to below his mouth, and white age pouches under his eyes. He sported a thick gray mustache, too heavy for his face, and his gray-flecked eyebrows sprouted schizophrenically above his sockets. He had two warts on his face, one on his chin, the other, sadly, on the end of his nose. If he had worn a dark wig and a black pointy hat and shaved his mustache, he'd have looked like Broom Hilda.

My mother, by contrast, was a looker with blonde hair (though she wore wigs), a dark, smooth complexion from tanning, high cheekbones, straight teeth, a good figure, an erect posture from years of carrying books on her head. She had been a model and even briefly ran her own modeling agency and charm school. She was also a flirt, especially when she drank.

We moved to the Texas Panhandle so that Buz and my mother could open a barbecue restaurant. During the move from Houston to Amarillo, Buz drove the U-Haul. My mother, accompanied by my sister and our poodle, drove Buz's van, and I drove the Oldsmobile with Vince, Buz's thirteen-year-old son, riding shotgun to help keep me awake. We didn't have CBs, and this was decades before cell phones. By the time we got to Dallas, we were all separated. We reunited in the middle of the night on the highway somewhere close to Wichita Falls. Buz and my mother were on the shoulder of the road screaming at each other. I fell asleep at the wheel in Childress and nearly ran into a Dunkin' Donuts. Just as we arrived in Amarillo, the Olds overheated, steam pouring from the engine.

Omens.

The barbecue restaurant that my mother and Buz had purchased had been left in disarray by the previous owner, with unwashed dishes and half-full milkshake canisters still at the blender. We never made any real effort to clean the place. My mother and Buz spent most of the time arguing. Within the month, they gave up on the whole enterprise and, after a period of unemployment, got jobs at a Pizza Inn: he as the night manager, she as a waitress. By that time, I was working at the movie theater and trying to adjust to sharing my room with a stepbrother I'd met only two days before the move.

By the spring of that year, things had further deteriorated. Buz and my mother drank heavily and stayed out late at nightclubs. Often he would return early, my mother sometime later. Though generally amiable, Buz, when he drank, had a temper. He was also a jealous man. I remember coming home from the movie theater many nights to find him sitting in the darkened living room, staring into the fireplace, poking the burning wood, a half-empty bottle of Jack Daniels and a glass on the hearth.

Buz began to scare me. He kept guns in the closet. I feared that something awful might happen in the house. At night, when my mother would arrive home, there would be fierce shouting matches that would draw Vince, Brandy, and me to the hallway, wondering what we should do. Buz would emerge from the room, his eyes bloodshot, his hair tousled, smiling, urging us back to our rooms. These episodes created tension between Vince and Brandy and between Vince and me. One day that winter, my sister told me that Vince had slapped her, and the next day I kicked him in the head and told him if he ever touched her again, I would kill him.

Later that spring, on a warm night, the same scenario occurred: my mother out, Buz poking the fire, the rest of us asleep. I woke to a crash and then a piercing scream. Vince and I rushed to the hallway, where my sister stood in my mother's doorway screaming. She held the poodle, who was barking madly. Buz was atop my mother on the bed with his fingers around her throat. I leapt on Buz, pinned him down, and began pummeling his disoriented and drunken face. My mother was by my side, screaming, "Kill him! Kill him!" Mascara streaked her cheeks. And then she suddenly jumped from the bed.

Buz and I both looked over, as if we had been merely wrestling in a fun-loving way, and saw my mother dragging Vince by the hair away from the closet. He held one of Buz's guns in his hands. My sister shrieked again and then darted out of the house with the dog. Suddenly, my mother, Buz, Vince, and I all stopped what we were doing, looked at each other in an embarrassed silence, and then went in search of my sister and the poodle.

Neighbors must have called the police because they soon were there, separating each of us into different rooms to hear our versions of the story, calling my uncle to come take my sister, Vince, and me away while the dispute was sorted out. I didn't want to leave our house, fearing what would happen to my mother if I left her alone with Buz. I was angry and confused and filled with so much adrenaline I couldn't sleep that night.

My uncle made us go to school the next day, but I skipped out after first period and went home. The house seemed serene in the daylight. Buz's van and my mother's car were in the driveway. When I opened the door, the house was eerily silent, and I dreaded what I might find. I could see my mother and Buz's bedroom door ajar at the end of the hall.

I walked slowly to it and inched it open enough to see inside. The wreckage from the night was still there—the broken lamp, the curtain rod dangling loose, ripped clothing scattered about the room, the torn bedspread on the floor. Buz and my mother were passed out on the bed, naked, their bodies entwined, a near empty bottle of Jack Daniels on the floor, the dog curled up on the end of the bed.

I stared for a long time from the doorway, wondering if perhaps they were dead, if this was some absurd suicide pact, poodle included. Then my mother, sensing my presence, slowly opened her eyes. She didn't move, didn't say a word, just stared at me. I stared back for a long time, too stunned to move. And then, feeling as if we had shared a sickening secret, I left the house.

When I came back later that day, Buz's and Vince's things were gone, as were they. I never saw or heard from them again.

3.

That summer that I flew into the lake at Medi-Park with Adam and Matt, only a month or so after Buz and Vince left, I lucked into a job as a bar-back at The Western Club, a country-western bar on the outskirts of Amarillo. My mother worked as a waitress there. She talked the manager—an obese, red-headed man named Mickey who was in love with her—into hiring me, even though I was only sixteen. She warned me that if I got caught by the Texas Liquor Commission, The Western Club would be shut down.

It was a great job, one that inspired awe among my friends. I was essentially the bartender's gofer. I washed glasses, refilled the soda gun tanks, kept the beer cases stocked, cleaned the counter, emptied the trash. This was around the time that the John Travolta and Debra Winger movie, *Urban Cowboy*, hit theatres. Country-western nightclubs in Texas were hot, especially if they had a mechanical bull, which The Western Club did. It was a huge place, with three separate bars, the bullring with mats all around to cushion the falls of drunken cowboys, a stage for the band, and a sawdust-covered dance floor. I wore a straw cowboy hat, pulled down low over my eyes, to help disguise my youth. During the rushes, I worked at such a frenzied pace that sweat poured from my hair, and my clothes were drenched. The Western Club was hopping every night, crammed so full that several times we were cited by the fire marshal for occupancy code violations.

I worked with two experienced bartenders, men who relished the kind of money that could be made at a nightclub like this. They shared their tips generously with me, and throughout the night they would pour shots of tequila for my mother, me, themselves, and my mother's younger brother, who also worked there that summer. We were usually pretty drunk by two in the morning, when the club shut down.

One night after we had closed, my mother offered to lock up so the other waitresses, bouncers, and bartenders could head over to the IHOP for breakfast. After they left, my mother took me to the liquor closet and walk-in cooler. She and I gathered several cases of beer, as well as unopened bottles of bourbon, tequila, and vodka, and carried them out to the trunk of a yellow Trans Am that one of the men in love with my mother that summer had lent us. After we loaded up the trunk with our stash, we swallowed another shot of tequila, and then she tossed me the keys and told me to drive.

We opened the top. I cruised the long stretch to I-40 and got on the interstate. The highway was desolate. My mother urged me to see how fast this puppy could go. I gunned it, past sixty, then seventy, eighty, and then ninety. Nervous, my eyes a little bleary from the wind and tequila, I started to taper off, and she asked me what the hell I was doing.

"Let 'er rip!"

I accelerated again until the speedometer hovered around a hundred. The wind whished over our heads, and my mother put her hand on top of her wig to keep it from blowing away.

"Step on it!" she shouted.

We screamed down I-40 into the heart of Amarillo. She reached her leg over and pressed her foot on top of mine so we'd go even faster. She laughed wildly. We edged past 110 mph. I gripped the steering wheel, and then my stomach shot into my throat as we flew past a policeman, who immediately turned on his flashers and sped after us.

I began slowing down, but my mother shouted, "Don't stop!" Seconds later, she screamed, "Get off here, get off here!" and pointed to an exit.

I wheeled the Trans Am off the ramp, still going nearly seventy miles an hour. The stolen beer and liquor bottles clanked in the back. "Turn here," she said. She directed me into an alley, where, following her orders, I stopped the car and shut it off. "Flip off your headlights!" All this maneuvering probably only took half a minute or so but seems, even now, long and vivid in my memory. We huddled in the seats and listened to the siren as it approached and then roared past the alley where we hid.

My mother and I had our knees on the floorboard, our faces close together on the vinyl seats. Our breaths whistled. Her wig was askew, and one of her false eyelashes was plastered to her cheek like an insect. My body shook, my blood thumping wildly in my neck and temples. She smiled, a big enough smile for me to see lipstick smudged on two of her top teeth.

"Now that's what I call fun," she said.

4.

The next summer, between my junior and senior year, when I was seventeen, I lived with my father in Las Vegas. I had called him months earlier, desperate to escape Amarillo. He told me to get a lifeguard's certificate and then fly out to Nevada to spend the summer with him. He said he would get me a job as a pool boy at one of the casinos, maybe even Caesar's Palace.

The job never materialized. Instead, I spent the summer floating in his apartment complex pool, walking the suburbs of Las Vegas, reading Ralph Waldo Emerson's essays, and plotting a new and more wholesome future for myself. I rarely spoke to anyone, not even my father, though the silence was not, after a while, awkward. He spent most nights downstairs with his girlfriend, a stewardess-turned-dental hygienist, a thoughtful woman who recommended books to me and read my sad, self-pitying poetry and, in general, gave me the distance I longed for without making me feel unwanted. Those three months were a strange and wonderful time of solitude and reflection, an ironic place for a monkish retreat. It was, I knew then and still believe now, a transformational summer, the turning point in my life. Had my father not granted me that time, had he not encouraged me to loaf and read and dream, I know I would have soon been, like most of my family, married with kids, working some crappy job, foregoing college, and resenting my life.

The first week I spent with my father in Las Vegas, however, was not so benign. I was still secretly popping black mollies, and I felt betrayed that he had not come through with the glamorous pool boy job. Perhaps most humiliating to me, his apartment was so small that we were forced, until he started sleeping downstairs with his girlfriend, to sleep together in his bed. (He had only a loveseat, too small for either of us, in his living room.) I had not seen my father in two years, and I felt that he had abandoned my sister and me. He was, in essence, a stranger. I had also just read *Moby Dick* in school, and I felt like Ishmael bedding down with Queequeg his first night in New Bedford, wondering if the tattooed cannibal might eat him.

My father snored heavily, something he denied when I was younger until my mother, sister, and I recorded him foghorning his way through a nap. That first week in Las Vegas, unable to sleep through the noise, I scrutinized him while he slept, something that I'm not proud of when I look back on it. It seems inhospitable, invasive, downright rude. But teenagers are not polite creatures. He was thirty-nine then, tanned, his skin freckled and starting to pucker and sag with sun and age. He'd lost some of the belly he had when he and my mother were married, but he still possessed a good-sized gut that looked ripe enough to thump. The wrinkles etched around his eyes and lips and crosshatched on his forehead disappeared while he slept, except for tiny creases as light as pencil lines. His upper lip vibrated when he snored, his teeth slightly yellowed and rimmed with nicotine stains. Three parallel wrinkle lines ringed his neck, like garroting marks, and his Adam's apple was not as prominent as in the pictures of him as the skinny kid who married my mother. A few hairs sprouted from his ears. He was handsome enough during the day—or so his girlfriend insisted: "Your father is a *very* sexy man, you know!" But at night that first week in Las Vegas, as I furtively watched him, I felt a little unnerved by what age could do to a man's body.

At seventeen, my body was, except for the excruciating pimples that I monitored with the vigilance of a prison guard, as athletic and smooth and taut as it would ever be. Though tall, I was still a boy in many ways, relatively hairless but muscled and immune to the effects of drugs and junk food. I found myself wondering if my body would grow into my father's. In the pictures of him as a young man, he was thinner than me, goofy-looking with jug ears and freckles. I marveled at the transformation and half-worried that in another twenty years this is what I had to look forward to: my own children examining my ossifying body while I warbled like a whale in my middle-aged sleep.

Soon enough, we worked out our routine for the summer. He moved downstairs, and I had his apartment to myself. I forgot all about those early awkward nights and began to enjoy the desert solitude.

At the end of the summer, I returned to Amarillo. Things had changed there as well. Adam had by this time left for Colorado and the fate that awaited him in the mountains. While I was in Las Vegas, my mother had declared herself a new woman and married her sixth husband, a man who made fiberglass port-a-potties. I seldom saw Matt and, in fact, went out of my way to avoid him. I was ready for a new life, a transcendental life promised me by my father and Emerson.

I saw my father only a few more brief times before he died, four and a half years later, of a massive heart attack. When I flew to Las Vegas for his funeral and viewed his body in the casket, I suddenly recalled those early paranoid evenings in his apartment, scrutinizing his body with that peculiar mixture of adolescent curiosity and contempt. Except for his warbling snore and the rise and fall of his chest, it was like I was just watching him again while he peacefully slept.

I am now the same age my father was when he died, a fact that both comforts and confounds me. I don't know how a quarter of a century has gone by. More baffling to me is the fact that I have four children, and that my eldest, a boy who looks so much like my younger self that he seems to inhabit my teenage body, will be sixteen soon.

And I have become that snoring man.

III

The Couple Upstairs

Upstairs, the body builder and his girlfriend go at it again and again with the window open. She's a moaner, her screams heard not only by us downstairs but by the whole apartment complex. God, she's loud. And so small compared to the protein-powdered bulk of him. She has a girl's body, smaller than my wife's, slender hips, knobby sticks for legs, unripe plums for breasts, a thin slash of a mouth. And him. Ouch! He's huge, I tell you, much bigger than me. Pectorals like cellophaned beef, massive arms the size of thighs. He shaves his head to define the musculature of his skull.

My wife and I have only been married seven months now. We're new to this city, both of us in grad school. We've been listening to them; we can't help it. Their bedroom's over our living room, the walls thin. At first we laughed about it. Yes, we were fascinated. The disparity in their sizes! *Geez*. Poor girl. Who could help but imagine it? Her legs spread wide like tiny twigs, his piston-chugging hips, all those dumbbells positioned like a grandstand around the bed, a huge metal audience watching what we've listened to. Then he goes on and on, that headboard banging away, the free weights sometimes dropping from their long bars, clattering over us like an earthquake, shaking the building. We've half-expected the ceiling to split open, their bed to crash down into our dinner.

I confess: it's gotten to me, made me envious and insecure in a way I'm ashamed to admit. Sometimes I've wanted us to just drop whatever we're doing—cooking dinner, grading lab reports, examining snake tissue under the microscope in our kitchen—and duplicate their feats, let this whole apartment building become one vibrating bundle of sweaty genitalia. But that hasn't happened. Even though we're newly married and reasonably proud of our own lovemaking, their carnal thrashing has made us shy with each other, embarrassed, their persistence and stamina a rebuke.

Now it's gotten old, and my wife and I have begun to detest them. *Shut your goddamn window!* I've wanted to shout. *Show a little courtesy, why don't you. Some people have to study!* We've had to learn to just wait it out—the pounding, the moans that eventually crescendo into her dog-like yelps—and carry on with what we have to do, and then it'll be over, and we can have some peace until the next round begins. But it's difficult.

Give it a break, I want to tell them. *Read a book. Go to the museum.*

Tonight we hear them at it again, just after dinner, like clockwork. At first it seems the same: the banging, the bed screeching, the thunder on the ceiling. So I tune them out, only half-listen. I'm studying the feeding habits of Asiatic reptiles, not easy work, but then I begin to sense a difference—the rhythm of the headboard, for one, and something in their muffled voices.

"Hey, listen to this," I say. "Something's happening."

"Don't," my wife says.

"No, it's different this time."

My wife lifts her head from her swollen mass of lecture notes, reports, and secondary sources. She listens, and then nods. "Yeah," she says, "you're right. I hear it."

"Go get a glass," I say.

"We shouldn't."

"This is important."

She brings one. I slide it over the wall to find just the right spot, like a medical student fumbling with a stethoscope. And yes, I do hear it. Something has definitely changed.

"Let me have a turn," my wife says. She adjusts the glass. "Flip off the lights so we can hear better," she says.

She's right. The darkness helps us concentrate.

I get another glass. There's a shift in the rustling of the bed sheets, in the violent duet of their bodies, then in the *shwoosh* of her feet on the floor. He plops down on his bench, removes the bar from the rack, lifts it heavily, grunting, frustrated. They speak in muffled hushes. They move to the other room, whispering, and we hear only snippets of sound as they move.

"Oh Jesus..." he says.

"Bullshit," she says. "That's not it... at all."

We follow them, like sea creatures beneath their boat, until we're in our bedroom, under their living room, and we find the right frequency.

"What was that?" the body builder asks.

"What do you mean?"

"You know what I'm talking about."

"I thought you'd like it."

"That's not the point," he says.

"So you did like it?"

There's a hard, flat quality to the girlfriend's voice that frightens me. Then they're quiet. We hold our breaths.

"Do you love me?" he asks.

My wife and I exchange surprised glances. Who would have thought this was about love? Silence again. We slide the glasses carefully. I miss something, but then I'm back.

"It's true then," he says. "Don't lie to me."

"I'm not lying," she says. But I can tell she's being insincere.

"Don't lie," he begs. "Please. I know."

A long pause. My heart flutters furiously, like a caught bird. Then nothing. Like a switch flipped off.

"What's going on?" I whisper.

"I don't hear anything."

We search intently across the wall, my face close to hers, lips almost touching, the ends of the glasses enclosing our ears.

"Me, either," I say.

"Sshhh," she whispers. "Close your eyes."

I move my glass.

"No," my wife whispers. "Just listen."

I imagine them on the couch, her small body curled up, her pony-tailed head nestled like a football in the crook between his chest and arm. There's only silence between them.

"Do you hear it?" my wife says.

"What?"

"Hold your breath," she says. "Listen."

I do as she instructs.

Yes, yes. My wife is right. I hear it, beyond the silence. Like those trick paintings where the image leaps forth from a mass of dots if you just relax and stare. It gets louder, a whine vibrating the walls. But what is it?

In the semi-darkness of the bedroom I can tell my wife has her eyes closed, concentrating. I close mine, tune in again. This sound, perhaps it is the silence itself, thickens and blooms, a low sad whistle almost too much to bear. Then it hits me. A shiver whips through my body. It's *him*, the body builder. *He's* making the sound. He's *crying*.

When I open my eyes, it's darker in our bedroom, but I clearly see tears glistening on my wife's cheeks, droplets of water hanging on either side of her chin, like iridescent globes. She's staring at me.

I place my tongue on the left side of her cheek, taste wet salt. She doesn't flinch. I put my open mouth on the other side, underneath her face, and wait until a drop falls on my tongue. I'm surprised by its weight, a rich watery disk. We set down the glasses, but we still hear him. It's loud now, a persistent buzzing. Scary.

My wife unbuttons my shirt, removes my jeans, deftly slips from her own clothes. She presses onto me. I can still hear him, as if he's dripping into our bedroom. The sobs grow louder and mingle with my wife's breathing. Though I'm inside her, I feel she's inside me somehow. It's very dark in the room, warm, the air thick, suffocating. Her red hair covers my face, and it's wet, from sweat or from tears, I don't know which. She presses harder, seems to grow on top of me, to take on more mass and density. My eyes roll heavily in their sockets. A rumble begins inside me, the start of a seizure. I want to make some sound, but I can't find my voice, can't even breathe.

I love my wife, I do, but all I can think of now is the way a python squeezes its prey, keeps constricting its reticulated body, methodically, before swallowing the animal whole.

First Birth

And what of the long startling transformation of your body and the way your stomach grows hard and round and enormous with rolling elbows and knees beneath the skin and the way your stomach stretches taut over the growth and turns red and purple and silver with striations and your belly button pops out and your breasts bulge from your bra and are rock hard and hot and too tender to touch and your hair grows long and wild like a chia plant. Remember the strange newness of that first pregnancy with both of us fascinated by the changes as we charted the growth with books and *NOVA* videos and during all the pregnancies that followed but especially that first one it was both disorienting and amazing to watch your body transform into something so alien from what we'd both known. Remember your exhaustion in those first few months as if your sleepiness was a backpack you struggled to carry but the second term you seemed full of energy and the final months you turned inward to the rhythms of the baby as the Braxton Hicks contractions interrupted the flow of each day like stop signs on a freeway and then the last week we were too ready for the end wishing for the final push but also a new flurry of anxiety and excitement trying to reconstruct our home and then the final days never knowing when it might come and the false starts and on-call readiness of our lives moved everything gradually and then very suddenly to the periphery until when we least expected it the labor arrived like God saying *It's showtime.*

I remember waiting as long as we could and then driving across the Cooper River Bridge in the middle of the night with no traffic and the lights of the city winking and the water churning up phosphorescence below and how we made the birthing room ours with your music and you were hungry for a pizza and thirsty for a cherry Coke and I remember taking you to the bathroom a hundred times and each time you had a contraction and we would laugh about it between the intervals of pain. Remember groping your way through the contractions silently closing your eyes and the midwife and the nurses amazed at your control compared to the woman in the room down the hall screaming horrendously as her baby mauled her and near the end I had to grip your leg when it began to shake uncontrollably as if all the jitters in your body had convened there for a committee meeting and you asked me to stroke your face with a cool rag as the contractions grew in strength and I tried to remain calm but frightened because it made me think of that story by Hemingway where the Indian woman struggles to have her baby and in the bunk above the husband slits his throat because he can't bear her screams.

    And then your sister finally showed up that next morning and remained distant from the action at first sitting in her chair reading a magazine until the pushing began and she had to be enlisted to hold your leg and the sun came through the window that morning bright and hot like a spotlight and between contractions you reminded me to call work and tell them I wasn't coming in and I remember so vividly your exhaustion that final hour and the way you would shake your head back and forth and back and forth deliriously and say *It burns it burns* and then the midwife cut you and the blood gushed onto the towels and the baby's head crowned like a huge red and white bowling ball and I wondered fleetingly if I'd ever want you in the same way after seeing this as if in the future this image would flutter in my mind like a ghost and dissolve my passion and then you jolted me back with a shout and then grunted loudly during the pushing and you weren't sure if you could go on but then almost as soon as you would say you'd had enough you'd contract your body for an interminable minute and this strange creature strained against the opening like a huge malleable chunk of wet clay and then suddenly his head was out.

    I remember that first ghoulish vision of him with his face trapped between your legs and your giddiness when you touched his forehead and him blinking and moving his nose like an old man but stuck there like a contorted vision from a sci-fi movie and then the final *push push push push* until the huge-bodied rest of him slithered out in one long heave and your sister's cartoon bug eyes popped from her sockets and you let out a long howl of combined joy and *labor*.

    I remember too my own shock at what I'd just seen as my eyes blurred hotly and this baby (our boy) suddenly wriggled on your stomach and you laughed and cried simultaneously saying *He's so beautiful he's so beautiful* as the thick glistening blue and white rope stretched from his stomach into you and then the midwife thrust the big scissors in my hand and told me to cut and I was unprepared for the thickness of the cord and the way it didn't slice on my first try but just slipped off the blades and when I did succeed purple jelly sprayed from both ends until she clamped them shut and I remember the flurry of activity afterwards as they stitched you up and then we made phone calls and you began nursing our son with his little mouth rooting immediately and hungrily for the colostrum and then after a while everybody left and we were alone together for the first time with him in the world and we both cried and you prayed and though I didn't I understood for the first time the meaning of grace as something given without deserving and it seemed and still seems to me now as if that moment was attached to our wedding night like two bright beads on a string or as if that original moment had led inevitably to this one and the way we felt on our wedding night crying joyously had somehow brought this baby into the world after a seven-year gestation and this was a secret passageway leading even deeper into the center of our lives and what we had made together would with good fortune now outlast us and it was just so damned astonishing to think *This is how the world works.*

When Our Son Died of Leukemia

The rubber-soled shoes of the nurses squeaked on floors mopped three times each day by an old Italian woman who seemed afraid of us, afraid of the eyes of parents in our wing.

We ate cafeteria sandwiches draped limply with lettuce. That last week, we didn't sleep. Our eyes bled sulfur. Our bitten nails snagged on the white afghan my mother had given us for our wedding. Each night flickered in the mute television set. The iron lung encasing the little girl across the hall from us whined insidiously. Then, suddenly, the girl and the machine were gone. No one warned us.

My wife counted the drops of solution as they beaded their way from the bag to the tube to the delicate crook of his arm. We had no words for this. I didn't think we would ever have words for this.

When he woke for the last time, his eyelids stuck together with gluey sleep. We wiped them with a warm blue washcloth we brought from home until he could see us. His eyes glittered like green stones in a shallow riverbed. And then, too soon, we closed his eyes. My wife kissed his vaselined lips. I ran my fingertips over his head, the veins at his temples visible through the skin which had turned, over the weeks, into milky glass.

    Outside the hospital, we were surprised by the summer heat, the smell of saguaro and the crackle, like static, of the cicadas. We stood in the buffalo grass and volcanic rock and watched the sun—bloody, gold, shimmeringly close—boil into the desert.

What They Didn't Tell You About the Vasectomy

1.

The Sunday before Christmas, when the white strip turns blue, as you both know it will, you feel the way you did when you heard the news of your father's death: a tingling numbness in your hands, up your arms, over your chest and face. You weep. Big baby sobs—heaving, moaning, keening, a real theatrical production. You're not proud of this behavior.

2.

You had hoped that this part of your life—bringing babies into the world—was over. Your oldest daughter, at six, demonstrates signs of self-sufficiency that raise your spirits. She can fix cereal, get dressed, brush her teeth. She reads now, too, and entertains herself with books or a drawing pad. She can even serve as a semi-responsible babysitter while you and your wife work at the kitchen table or on the computer. Your son has speech difficulties and, at four, is slow with toilet training, but has made great strides recently. The thirteen-month-old, another girl, is fierce, trouble in the making.

You have heard parents claim that adolescence is the hard part. "You're in the easy stage," they tell you. You resent their condescension, their smugness. They suffer from amnesia. The first five years are a killer. Irregular sleep patterns, anxious vigilance. The whole house a baby-proofed war zone. Every mouth-sized item in the house must be moved out of range: you call it "raising the standard of living." An era of diaper blow-outs, leaking breasts (*off-limits to you, mister*), spit-up stains, projectile vomiting, complicated logistics just to get out the door, everything rigorously timed around naps and nursing schedules. Your wife falls asleep before, and sometimes while, making love.

The pea-sized fetus in her womb is another domestic explosion, twenty more years before you can have your life back, if you can ever have it back. When your father died, the doctors said, "His heart exploded."

Another baby will, you think, explode yours.

3.

Your wife tries to comfort you but really wishes you'd just get over it. She's happy; you know she's happy. Your sorrow saddens but does not surprise her. Despite the way the babies scar her body, she would have ten children if you would let her. She has to muzzle her joy, keep private her gratitude for the resurrection of her uterus.

Though you have tried to prevent another baby from coming, your wife will not, now that the deed is done, interfere with the process. Those are her words: *Interfere with the process.* You appeal to her environmental ethic. A fourth child will make you 2PR: Two Past Replacement. She's not buying it.

She, too, is exhausted, the youngest still nursing. Nevertheless, she'll have this baby. She's dreamed about having more help with the chores, though. A friend of hers said she gave up her shrink for a housekeeper, and it was the best trade she ever made.

Your wife brings in a modest income as an environmental consultant and non-profit grant writer, but neither of you can afford a shrink. You gave yours up long ago, when you were broke and struggling as an actor in New York. Your paychecks are sporadic at best. Your wife says she loves that you're an actor, would never dream of telling you to give it up, but talent, she reluctantly reminds you, doesn't pay the bills. You got lucky with a few national commercials that continue to bring in residuals, and you pick up enough gigs doing repertory theatre, radio and television spots, reading books on tape, and teaching private workshops to help you get by. You've managed to call yourself, without too much irony, a working actor, which is all you've ever aspired to be. More babies threaten even that humble dream.

4.

"Buck up," she croons in your ear. "It's not that bad. No birth control for the next eight months."

You hop from the couch and sprint down the hall.

"Where are you going?"

You rummage through the bathroom drawer. You will do what you promised—*threatened*—to do. You return with a steel bowl, matches, some lighter fluid, and the plastic case containing the cervical cap, a device you never trusted.

"You're not really going through with it, are you?"

"You bet I am." You open the case and dump the cap into the bowl, douse it with the lighter fluid.

"Don't be such a drama queen."

You strike the match.

"Any last words?" you ask.

"Goodbye, old friend."

"Traitor," you say and drop the match.

"You're going to burn the house down."

"What do I care?" Tears stream down your cheeks.

"Honey, it's going to be fine."

You watch the flame wither, the cap only half-burned, black crust around the edges.

"It stinks," she says.

You strike another match, drop it in. The smoke alarm shrieks. Seconds later, your oldest stands, shaking, at the end of the hallway. Your wife comforts her and tells her to quiet the others, who howl from their room.

You stare at the reflection in the bowl: your face sodden and puffy, your hair a mess. Though not quite thirty-three—the year of your martyrdom, you think—you suddenly look fifty.

"Nice job, honcho," your wife says, shaking her head.

5.

For the duration of the pregnancy, your wife doesn't want to hear about permanent birth-control options.

"Bad *juju*," she says.

She thinks love is a renewing fountain, an endless geyser, an inexhaustible gift. Your metaphor is miserly, fraught with the calculus and fallacy of conservative economics.

After months of holding a grudge, you try to align yourself toward your wife's vision of love, to lean into the light, as she says. It ain't easy.

6.

But when the baby comes—after twenty-nine hours of labor, she slithers effortlessly into the midwife's hands—what else can you do but adore her, a quiet, healthy infant, who looks like you, dark-headed and swarthy. The other children seem like your wife's progeny: reddish hair and pencil-thin eyebrows, skin the color of skim milk.

This child sleeps through the night. She is perfect. You call her the Danger Baby. One look at her, friends and relatives say, and they want another child themselves. You know your wife and this baby are in cahoots. *Let's show him how easy it is. Then you won't be the last.*

7.

When the midwife gives the okay to make love again, you're wary. You declare official war against your testicles. You think of your sperm as a sneaky battalion, plotting ways to rebuild the bombed bridge, to jump the chasm, to strike with sniper precision. Your sperm are more powerful than cervical caps, condoms, and diaphragms. Guerrilla soldiers trained in the boot camp of evolution to penetrate your wife's ova.

Spermicidal, that's how you feel. You half-joke about cutting the whole sack off, heaving the bloody spectacle with its potent billions to the coyotes that traipse across your yard.

8.

"I have a hole in my nutsack that still hasn't healed," says a friend, a vasectomy veteran with five children whose testimonial you have sought. "Keeps scabbing over."

"You do what you want," another friend tells you when you broach the subject over margaritas and a baseball game. "I'm not letting anybody near my balls with surgical instruments."

"Would you rather your wife get her tubes tied?" you ask.

"Better her than me."

9.

You throw a poker party, invite buddies who you know have done the deed, plus several holdouts. When you steer the conversation toward vasectomies, your friends are a Greek chorus, strophe and antistrophe.

"The peace of mind is *so* worth it."

"What about the quality of orgasm?"

"I can't tell any difference."

"Well, I could. For about the first year, it wasn't as dramatic, if you know what I mean. Like someone siphoned off the gasoline."

"Depends on the position. If I'm on bottom, I can't quite blow my stack."

"What about pain?" you ask.

"I had mine done Monday afternoon, and by Wednesday morning I was back at work."

"Did you hear about Rawlings, the guy with the landscaping business? He was on a riding mower the next day and—*whew*—talk about a mess!"

"Torval says Lizzie and Terry are the result of botched vasectomies."

"Did he have them done in Tijuana?"

"Just some badass luck, and you're stuck with four kids instead of two."

"At first, I felt this popping whenever I came. Scared me half to death. Then it just went away. Or maybe I just don't think about it anymore."

"I don't know, man," says your best friend, a philosophy professor at the local Jesuit college. He's remained suspiciously quiet. "If you cut off the source, there will be consequences."

"Physical?" you ask.

"Physical, moral, emotional, spiritual, psychological, you name it. Bad news. Once you make this decision, you can never go back. You won't be a man anymore. I don't care what kind of reversal they're promising in Phoenix or Houston. You'll never even have the *possibility* of another child."

"But if you don't want another kid?"

"You never know. You're only thirty-three. What happens if you're another Job, and your family, God forbid, is wiped out?"

"What the hell? Don't even talk like that!"

"I'm just saying. . . . Or what if, in another twenty years, in your second or third marriage—"

"Shut up!"

The comedian says soberly, "I heard it can lead to prostate cancer."

"Don't listen to those horror stories," the tax attorney argues. "Your sex life will be better than ever. No rubbers, no worries. Peace of mind—pleasure and peace of mind."

"You'll be a eunuch," the professor says.

10.

After the long last labor, your wife has done an about-face. She gobbles up your anecdotes and interviews, though she dismisses the horror stories. She does some research, provides statistics that prove how easy the procedure is, especially compared to the alternatives for women. She gives you a gray three-ring binder. The notebook has multi-colored tabs and contains documentation, statistics, testimonials, even poems. Vasectomy poems!

"It'll hurt," you say.

She raises her eyebrow, folds her arms. "I delivered four babies, buster."

11.

You do not read anything inside the gray three-ringed binder with multi-colored tabs.

12.

At a follow-up visit to the midwife, your wife mentions permanent birth control options.

"That's your job," the midwife says to you. "After four kids, you don't *walk*, you *run* to the nearest urologist."

You suspect your wife has spoken to her in advance. You smell a conspiracy.

13.

The examination room at Dr. Oldini's office has a small combination TV/DVD player with a DVD about Viagra on top of it.

"Isn't *Oldini* a weird name for a urologist?" you ask your wife.

"How so?"

"It sounds like *Old Wienie*."

She doesn't find this funny.

Dr. Old Wienie turns out to be a lanky middle-aged guy with a dark tan and the kind of handsome wrinkles that inspire confidence. He wears white tube socks and reminds you of your high school football coach.

With deft authority, he explains it all: the simple plumbing, the miniature tools, the dissolving stitches, a minor procedure. He pulls down a screen attached to the wall and displays the cutaway illustration—like a *deferens* coordinator designing an attack. He points to incisions on either side of the droopy penis and speaks with real passion about his patented Triple Blitz of Snip-Staple-Cauterize that will keep the millions from jumping the chasm.

Like your wife, he dismisses the naysayers and horror stories, the faulty studies linking the procedure to prostate cancer, the superstitions about a vasectomy ruining your libido.

You ask him about operations gone awry.

"Nonsense," he says. "I've performed over four hundred and never had a bad one yet. Believe me, it'll be the best decision of your life."

You feel a little better now, bolstered by Old Wienie's authority, the evidence of his Triple Blitz technique. But you're not completely sold. You'd like to wait a while longer, mull it over.

"You in?" he asks.

Your wife says, smiling: "He's in, and he's in to win."

14.

You arrange to visit a cattle ranch just outside of town. You tell the rancher you're researching for a role in a film, and you want to see them castrate the calves.

"You're in luck," the rancher tells you. "We're castrating and branding next Tuesday."

The process is efficient and cruel. The calves are led into a long, tight chute, the rancher's wife surprisingly gentle. "Come on, babies," she sings to them. "Come on now, that a way." She soothes them with her gloved hands. When a calf startles and tries to turn, one of the handlers grabs its tail, twists and pushes, until the calf moves along. "That a way, honey," the rancher's wife purrs.

The chute opens onto a special stainless steel table, the sides folded up at a ninety-degree angle. Two handlers strap the calf in and unfold the table. The brander pulls the glowing brand from the fire. When the calf bawls, your own testicles shrivel. The calf's tongue extends from its mouth, longer and flatter than you would have imagined.

Almost simultaneously, the handlers pull the legs back and hold the calf down so that the scrotum is exposed. The castrator, using a small sharp knife that he whets on a marble slab and dips into a Folgers can full of disinfectant, slits the sack from the top down, revealing an inner sack, which he also slits.

Two cylindrical, blue-gray glistening testicles suddenly protrude, the shape of large figs. The castrator jams his forked fingers upward and yanks down hard. A springy cord extends tautly from the calf's abdomen. The castrator snips the top of the cord. The calf's legs twitch a bit, but there's no sound, no obvious pain, as there was seconds ago with the branding. You wonder if the calf's in shock. The cord and most of the scrotum retract into the calf's body. Much less blood than you imagined.

The castrator tosses the testicles into a large plastic tub. The straps are released, and the calf runs free without any noticeable wobble. All of this takes less than a minute, and you watch each calf coming down the chute with a horrified awe. The smoke and the smell of branded flesh. You cover your nose and mouth with the bandana you brought. The rancher's young children, a girl and a boy, chase the seemingly unfazed calves.

"Isn't this cruel?" you ask the rancher's wife.

"They're just animals," she says, a sad, unsentimental love in her voice. "They don't know what's happening to them, and they don't worry about it afterward. Pain's not the same for them."

"How do you know that?"

"I've been doing this all my life."

The rancher walks over with a plastic bag full of bloody testicles. "You wanna take these home and fry 'em up?"

Your leg twitches. "What?"

"They're pretty tasty. Just soak 'em in salt water, rinse 'em, batter 'em, fry 'em in some canola oil."

"This is a joke, right?"

"They're a delicacy," the rancher's wife says, straight-faced. "Google it."

15.

"What are you doing with those things?" your wife asks.

"I'm going to eat them."

"That's sick."

"It's a delicacy."

"Is this some kind of whacked-out ceremony?"

"Of course not," you say innocently, raising the dripping testicles in your hands. "Calf fries. Rocky Mountain oysters."

"Why do you have to be so dramatic about everything?"

"Who's being dramatic?"

"I am *not*—I repeat, *not*—cooking them for you," she says on her way out of the kitchen.

You rinse the hair, blood, and gristle away, soak them in salt water, as directed, and rinse them again until they shine like the blue-gray glaze of a vase. You prepare a batter of eggs, cracker crumbs, a little bit of honey, and heat the oil in a cast iron skillet.

You hold two testicles, ready to roll them in the batter. They fit snugly in your palm, like tender worry stones. You cannot bring yourself to batter them yet. They seem vulnerable, beautiful even, glistening in your hands. You will not eat them now. You are not sure if you will ever be able to eat them. But you cannot throw them away either. So you put them in a freezer bag.

On the label, you write in big bold letters: <u>BALLS</u>.

Underneath, you write: "<u>Do Not Throw Away</u>."

And underneath that: "<u>I MEAN IT!</u>"

16.

The night before the surgery, you, as ordered, shave your scrotum. You sleep horribly that night. It feels as if ants are chewing your testicles. You try lotion, but that exacerbates the burn.

"Oh my God, honey," your wife says when she finds you sitting on the toilet seat, soaking your genitals in a bowl of ice water. "Why didn't you let me do that? I know how to shave sensitive areas."

"I didn't trust you."

"Well, you should have," she says, inspecting the damage. "Geez, you're nicked up pretty bad. Did you use any shaving cream?"

"I'm not a total fool," you say. All evidence to the contrary.

17.

Unfortunately, you know the nurse who assists Old Wienie. Her daughter goes to school with your eldest. You have volunteered together for car washes, rummage sales, and talent shows. She is slim and buxom, with a thick Texas twang and a rowdy sense of humor. She is overly impressed that you are an actor. You have flirted with her. You wish you could reschedule. You do not want this woman to see your poorly shaved scrotum.

"Just put this on," she says, handing you a hospital gown.

After undressing in the bathroom, you inspect yourself again. This is not good. To make matters worse, it's cold. Your penis shrivels.

"Ready?" she asks when you emerge from the bathroom. "Let's see what you got," she jokes and pats the leather medical table, draped in white tissue.

You laugh nervously.

"Oh," she says, shaking her head disapprovingly. "Looks like you sort of mangled the shaving."

"Sorry."

"Should have let your wife handle that. Well, not to worry. I can fix this, lickety-split."

She pulls out some green gel and a razor, quickly lathers your testicles, which she handles a little too roughly. In less than a minute, she's finished.

"Just let me put the disinfectant on," she says. The spray makes you flinch. "Don't worry. Everything'll be just fine." She wheels over a stainless steel tray. You see a long needle and a vial. You have never liked needles. You sometimes vomit and pass out at the mere sight of them. "Ready for some joy juice?" she asks.

"What is that?"

"Just a little something so you won't feel any pain."

"Where are you putting it?"

"In your penis."

"*What?*"

She laughs and slaps your thigh. "Ha! That gets 'em every time. Here, give me your arm. It won't hurt, I promise."

She's a liar. The needle does hurt. You can feel it burning under your skin.

"I'll give you a few minutes of alone time," she says, patting you on the knee, "to let the juice do its magic. And then we'll get started. Are you comfy?"

"Yes."

"Good. Dr. Oldini and I will be back before you know it."

18.

Popped my rocks.

That phrase bubbles up from your adolescence, the boasts of boys huddled together, the vulgar lyricism of Henry Miller and *Penthouse*. You remember, too, those candies that explode in your mouth, Pop Rocks, and the sound you could make with your index finger lodged inside your mouth, in the crook of your jaw, quickly released, a high-pitched hollow *pop*. After you learned that trick, you popped your jaw with your finger all day, your lips cracking at the corners, the inner lining of your cheek, once wet and smooth and warm, turning dry from overuse, calloused with ridges from your ragged fingernails. But you kept on. You couldn't stop, faster and faster, like a chant, your mother finally shouting: *Enough already!*

"You all right down there," Old Wienie asks, his face hidden behind a surgical mask.

You put your finger in your mouth and make the sound. "Pop!" you say to emphasize your point.

"Oh, yeah," the nurse says, "he's doing juuuuuust fine."

19.

The nurse has to help your wife get you to the car. You wobble. Your groin is wrapped in ice. On the drive home, you see Granite Mountain in the distance, smoke rising from the peak.

"What's that?"

"A controlled burn," your wife says. "I heard it on the radio."

"Where there's smoke," you shout, "there's fire!"

Your wife shakes her head. "Let's get you home."

You gaze dreamily out the window. You pass what you and your wife call the Mormon Billboard, which features an inspirational quote that changes each month.

You and your wife make fun of it because the quotes are often taken out of context. This month's quote is from Tennessee Williams, a decidedly non-Latter Day Saint: "I'VE ALWAYS DEPENDED ON THE KINDNESS OF STRANGERS."

Three years ago you played Stanley Kowalski at the Milwaukee Rep, one of the highlights of your career. You repeat the line for your wife, impersonating Blanche Dubois' drawl as she's escorted to the mental institution. "Stanley would never have allowed anyone near his balls!" you moan.

"Calm down there, Brando."

"A man should be king of his castle!"

At home, with jockstrap and icepack attached, the room spins. You need to piss, but you're not sure if you know how. You call for your wife, who helps you into the bathroom and pulls down the jock strap and the ice pack.

When you urinate, it dribbles and burns.

"You okay there, honey?"

You try to get up but pitch forward, your head landing in the trash can.

"You fainted," she tells you later. "Scared me to death."

You have to piss again, but that frightens you. It's an itchy, swollen mess down there. "More ice," you say. "Please."

"You know," your wife tells you when she returns with a fresh ice pack and another pill, "you are such a baby. Good thing *you* didn't have the babies."

"Good thing indeed," you echo, drifting off.

20.

You think you feel well enough to get out of the house. Your wife wants to go minivan shopping. No other vehicle, besides a tank or a bus, will hold your entire family. At the Minivan Emporium, the salesman asks what's wrong, and then nods empathetically when you explain.

"When I got my vasectomy," he says, "the doc accidentally snipped an artery. Later that day, my scrotum filled with blood. I had to have emergency surgery to stop the hemorrhaging."

This does not seem like a smart sales strategy.

"Can we go home?" you ask your wife.

21.

A week later, the pain has not subsided. Your prescription has run out. You still walk bow-legged. The stitches have not dissolved; they poke through your boxers. You do not like wearing boxers. You do not like being in pain. You cannot stop weeping. A eunuch, that's what you've become.

You call Old Wienie's office and ask for an appointment. ASAP.

"Okay, let's study the situation," he says. He slips on gloves, wheels the stool close to you and plops down so that his face is buried in the middle of your crotch. He still wears white tube socks. He nudges your penis to the side with one finger and lifts your swollen sack with his other hand. His touch is tender. You appreciate this.

"Looks just fine to me," he says.

"Shouldn't the stitches be gone by now?"

He's still cupping your scrotum. "Give it a week."

"What about the pain?"

"It lasts longer for some than others," he says, releasing you. "I was up and about in twelve hours."

This sounds like an indictment.

He hands you another prescription. "Come see me in four weeks."

22.

You are afraid of your body. The two erections you woke to earlier in the week made you yelp. So you have suppressed all thoughts that might trigger the pain. As a last resort, you think of the cord of each calf retracting into its abdomen, the twitch of each calf's leg. That usually does the trick, shrivels you fast.

But several days later, from bed, you watch your wife emerge from the misty shower, her skin flushed. She looks so lovely, even after four babies. You want her. You feel the heat in your groin, there's no stopping it now. You brace yourself but, miraculously, no pain. Your eyes glisten.

"What's wrong?" she asks, hooking her bra.

"Nothing. You just look so pretty."

"You're such a sentimental slob," she says and walks to your side of the bed. "Oh," she says, looking into your lap. "What's that?"

"A gift," you say.

"Any pain?"

"Not yet," you whisper.

23.

"Any problems?" Old Wienie asks at the next appointment.

"Just this popping sensation. Like something might be broken in there."

"Naaah," he says. "That's just in your mind."

"I'm sort of... worried," you stammer.

"Nothing to worry about, my friend. It's like any other muscle. You just need to get it back in shape. Use birth control for now, and then come back in for a specimen count in two weeks."

As you leave, you see another man about your age wobbling from the office, his wife and the nurse at his elbows. The man looks dazed. The poor eunuch.

24.

"What's the matter?" your wife asks a week later. Your head is buried in your hands.

What is there to say? Perhaps your friend was right. You have made a terrible mistake. You are no longer the king of your castle.

25.

It is hot and breezy the day before your specimen count. The wind rustles what few trees there are, alligator junipers with their mottled hide-like bark. For the last week, the monsoon season has thrashed your town with a flurry of lightning storms and floods that have ravaged the decomposed granite in your yard. The black plastic tarps, designed to keep weeds from taking over your lawn, are exposed now in spots that make the earth look dead underneath. The hail and winds have knocked over your barbecue grill, damaging the steel rods.

You find it odd that you worry about the storms' effects on your shoddy landscaping and cheap grill, the bourgeois trophies and hazards of your life. But there it is: you are simply an unemployed actor with four kids, a used minivan with ninety thousand miles on it, a ravaged yard, and a useless sack of sperm.

26.

You take the BALLS from the freezer, thaw them in the microwave, fry them until the batter turns brown and crispy. You dip them in honey mustard, wash them down with a glass of sweet iced tea.

"Daddy, Daaaaddy!" your two-year-old daughter calls from her crib.

"Look who's up?" you say, hoisting her into your arms. "You ready for a snack?"

27.

Later that night, your wife pulls out some fish to defrost for dinner and notices the freezer bag is missing.

"What happened to your—"

"I ate them for lunch."

28.

You feel slightly ashamed as you hand the nurse the clear plastic specimen jar, much too big for its contents. "I'm more prolific in the evening," you say, smiling to let her know it's a joke. She rolls her eyes. You feel your own inadequacy. This woman has shaved your scrotum.

"We'll call you this afternoon," she says.

"Will it take long?"

"No. I just need to check it under the microscope."

"Can I watch you do it?"

She looks around. Everyone's gone, presumably to lunch. "Sure, I guess so. There's a lull before the afternoon appointments. Come on back."

You follow her.

She slides the glass plate under the microscope. After adjusting the lens, she says, "Uh-oh."

"What's the matter?"

"How many times have you ejaculated since your surgery?" she asks.

"Thirty times," you say. "That's what Dr. Oldini recommended." You step closer to her.

"This is really odd. You should be clear by now. Maybe you haven't ejaculated enough," she says. "You need to flush them out."

"I've done it plenty of times. More than thirty. Definitely more."

"It takes longer for some men. Maybe you don't release as many at a time." She points to the slide. "There are a lot here. Maybe the deferens has grown back together. That's part of the risk, you know."

"But what about the Triple Blitz?" Your neck and temples begin to throb. "Snip-Staple-Cauterize. Dr. Oldini said he'd never had one go bad. I thought this was foolproof."

"Calm down."

"I *am* calm!"

"I understand your concern."

"What the hell is going on?"

"Please, keep your voice down."

"I'm sorry," you whisper.

"It can happen, that's all I'm saying."

"But it *never* happens to him! Over four *hundred* vasectomies. You were there. You heard him. He's the fucking *deferens* coordinator!"

"Please, do not raise your voice."

You take a deep breath.

"Yes, Dr. Oldini has a perfect surgical record," she says. "But maybe you're the—"

"What? I'm the *what*?"

"—anomaly."

"Anomaly? ANOMALY?"

"You seem to have more live sperm than when we tested you last time."

"Oh, this is great. You're telling me I'm a scrotal anomaly! That's classic! What happens now?"

"You can wait for Dr. Oldini. He should be back in the office any minute."

"And?"

"He may have to redo the vasectomy. I'm sorry—"

"Oh my God!" You feel very dizzy. You sit down, put your head between your knees. "How could this happen?"

"It does sometimes."

"No, it *never* happens to Old Wienie!"

She looks stunned by what you've called her boss.

"I'm sorry I got loud," you say. You are sorry. This woman has been nothing but considerate to you.

She pats your shoulder. "Are you okay?"

"Actually, I feel a little dizzy."

"Lie down here for a minute. I'll get you some water."

29.

Then she is by your side, her hand resting on your forehead. You feel that you have lost some time, passed out.

"There now," she says. "You better?"

"Yeah."

"I hate to ask you this—"

"What is it?"

"Can you come back tomorrow? Dr. Oldini just called. He's stuck at the hospital and won't return to the office today."

30.

Driving home, you feel lightheaded again. You see Granite Mountain in the distance. No smoke. No fire. *But there is a fire.*

You think of that poor sap wobbling out of the doctor's office. You do not want to go through that again. But what choice do you have?

You see a man reworking the Mormon Billboard. The first line of the quote is already up: "THE LIFE YOU HAVE IS YOUR INHERITANCE."

The man is pasting the second strip of the quote on the billboard. You're going too slow. Cars honk and whiz around you. "AND WHAT YOU DO WITH YOUR INHERITANCE" is all you see before you're past it.

What you do with your inheritance IS WHAT?

You keep driving. You'll see it plenty of times before they change it. You pass the sign every day when you take the kids to school. But the farther you go, the more you feel it calling you back, as if your life depends on finding out what it says. If your wife were with you, she'd accuse you of melodrama.

You turn at the next street and drive around the block. You pull off on the shoulder, get out, and watch the guy paste the final phrase on the billboard.

> THE LIFE YOU HAVE IS YOUR INHERITANCE.
> WHAT YOU DO WITH YOUR INHERITANCE
> IS THE POETRY OF YOUR LIFE.
>
> —Reverend C. B. Baxter

31.

"How'd it go?" your wife asks when you arrive home. She's on the bed nursing the baby. The two oldest are at school. The toddler is napping in the next room.

"Fine."

"Everything dead down there?"

"That's a cruel thing to say!"

She reaches for your hand. Her skin is soft. "I'm only joking. I thought that's what you wanted."

"It was."

"Well, then. Congratulations."

She gently dislodges the baby's mouth from her nipple. The baby's eyes are closed, but her lips move as if she's still nursing.

"Let's make love," you say.

Your wife laughs and says, "I have to go to work soon."

"We need to celebrate." You slip your shirt over your head.

"What about the baby?"

"Just leave her here beside us. We'll rock her to sleep."

Your wife lays the baby down and creates a cushion of pillows and blankets around her.

32.

"Daddy, Daaaaaaddy!" your two-year-old sings from her room. "I wake. Get me, get me."

"Daddy will be there in a minute, sweetie," your wife calls. And then to you, she says, "You better hurry."

"Daaaddy. Up! Up!"

"Yes, Daddy's up," your wife says.

"Don't make me laugh. I'm trying to concentrate here."

"DAAAAAAAADDY!"

You can hear her jumping in her crib, bouncing up and down on the mattress. The crib smacks against the wall dividing the rooms.

"Go help your daughter," your wife says.

"DADDY, DADDY, DADDY!"

"I'm coming."

33.

You hover above your wife. A glistening thread connects you to her, and you watch for a second as it stretches between you both, an ordinary miracle. You imagine, in that split-second, the contents of the luminous thread under a microscope, millions of tadpoles swimming in thin milk, their tails wriggling frantically. *Alive.*

Go, you think. *Go!*

You roll from the mattress and into your boxers as your wife drapes her arm around the baby and attaches the tiny lips to her breast.

"Thanks," your wife says.

You feel a delicious, traitorous thrill. If you touch anything, you're sure you'll see blue sparks.

She smiles, closes her eyes. "I'm gonna take a short nap. Wake me in twenty minutes, will ya?"

"Daddy, Daaaaaddy!" your daughter calls again, her voice more insistent, a touch of panic in it. And again the whack, whack, whack against the wall.

"You better go get her before she breaks the crib."

You think of the Mormon Billboard, of your inheritance, of the poetry of your life. What have you done?

Alive, you think. *Alive!*

You brush your wife's hair away from her face, kiss her lips, and then kiss the crease between the baby's cheek and your wife's breast. Your eyes burn.

"Hey," your wife says. "I thought your crying days were over."

You don't answer, just admire them both.

"Daaaaaddy, Daaaaaddy, Daaaaaddy!"

You start to speak, but can't. You breathe, in and out, in and out, until you feel your chest loosen. You drape the sheet over your wife and baby like a shroud.

"Daaaaaddy, Daaaaaddy, Daaaaaddy!"

You slip on your pants and head for the door.

"I'm on my way," you call, your voice a choked melody. "I'm on my way."

Love Song for the Quarantined

At dinner our youngest boy said he hoped it snowed because he wanted to sleep in the next morning. He was so tired. Blue circles shadowed his eyes. The following day, while his older brother and two younger sisters readied themselves for school, he lay in bed and refused to get up, so we let him stay home. He slept late the next morning as well, but then woke suddenly, gasping and coughing uncontrollably. My wife propped him up, stroked his back, calmed him until he caught his breath. She made a pallet in the living room and let him watch cartoons. By lunchtime he was hungry, a good sign, and he ate macaroni and cheese and some applesauce, gulped down a big glass of milk. When his brother and sisters returned from school, he was happy to see them, and that night they played several games of Slap Jack. He seemed better the next morning, more rested, but the cough continued, so we kept him home just to be safe. By the afternoon, he was not doing well at all.

The pattern continued. The third night was the worst. He couldn't catch his breath, and sometimes he coughed so hard his face darkened and he began to dry-heave.

"We've got to take him to the doctor," my wife said. "This is not good."

"Probably *pertussis*," our doctor told us. "Whooping cough."

"Wasn't he vaccinated for that?" my wife asked. She knew about these things.

"Sometimes the vaccination doesn't completely protect against it. We better get him on something and have him tested. Are your other kids showing symptoms?"

"No coughing, if that's what you mean."

We started him that night on the antibiotic. The next morning, I called the Health Department to set up an appointment for the test.

"He can't be tested once he's begun antibiotics. Your doctor should know that," the nurse said. She was agitated, a tinge of panic in her gravelly voice. "You're all going to have to go on antibiotics. If your other children or you or your wife show any symptoms, you must stay home. We had an outbreak in the county just last year, and it took us forever to get it under control."

"But only my son is sick," I said. "The rest of us are fine."

"For now," the nurse said ominously. "You have to start the medication. *Immediately.* We must be *vigilant*. I'm sorry to tell you this, but your family is now officially considered a community health risk. I will fax your kids' schools and your employers." And then she added, as if she were a parole officer, "We *will* call to check on you."

Our doctor wouldn't send the prescriptions to the pharmacist without seeing each of us separately, an expense that we couldn't afford. I called the Health Department and asked that they fax the prescription for the antibiotics, but the pharmacist said he was out of that particular antibiotic. He could get it in by the next afternoon.

"That's fine," I said.

That night, the house convulsed with coughing. Both my sons, my youngest daughter, and then me. Our lungs seemed to explode. Our daughter vomited once, twice, three times. My wife gave everybody a handkerchief and instructed us to cough into it and fold it over to keep the germs contained, but it was no use. I imagined the house glowing with the expectorated germs. My wife propped us up with pillows, applied cool cloths to our foreheads and the backs of our necks, cranked up the vaporizers, and administered cough syrup, which the children promptly threw up. She worried, I could tell, that it would be only a matter of time before she and our oldest daughter caught it.

By dawn, everyone looked shell-shocked. At eight, I called the Health Department and told them what had happened.

"Did you start the antibiotics?" asked the nurse.

"The pharmacist said the prescription wouldn't be ready until this afternoon."

"I'm sorry then," she said, "but your family is now officially under quarantine."

. . .

We understood sickness. Every winter or spring, sometimes both, a virus snaked through our home. No family our size could avoid it. We charted the years by our infections. Bronchitis Christmas, the St. Valentine's Day Strep Throat Massacre, the Easter Bunny Flu that wiped us out for a month. Winter ushers in a season of colds, and spring unleashes the ragweed and juniper allergies. And we catch it all.

However, we had been, we believed, through the worst. Not quite the worst, I know. But that's how we, my wife and I, liked to talk about it—*through the worst*—as if to ward off any similar occurrences. Five years ago, our oldest son developed cancer of the spleen, rare among children. The cancer nearly destroyed us. We took him to pediatric oncologists in Houston and Phoenix. He had three surgeries followed by harrowing months of experimental chemotherapy and radiation. He should be, by all odds, dead.

At the direst moments during that time, I could not sleep. Besieged by migraines, sometimes two a day, I was lucky if I got ten hours of sleep a week. I'd be giving a lecture about proprietary rights in contract law at the university where I teach, and my nose would start to bleed. At night, I'd roam the streets of our neighborhood, or walk to the all-night diner and read *Oncology*, the latest *New England Journal of Medicine*, or the articles I'd downloaded and printed from the internet.

My wife's hair turned a silvery blonde during the middle months of that period, even though she was only thirty-two. She and I and our other kids shaved our heads in solidarity with my son—an ultimately comical tribute that cheered him immensely. We bought wigs and party hats and threw a "bald party." You had to shave your head to attend; surprisingly, four of our friends and my wife's two brothers and father did. Even my son's Phoenix oncologist, who had taken a special liking to our boy and had written an article for a medical journal about the radically aggressive treatment for pediatric cancer of the spleen.

We had come through to the other side, and nothing could ever be quite as bad, we thought. No setback could touch us with the same horror.

"At least it's not the spleen," we would say, a comic mantra, determined to treat our near-tragedy lightly.

But I must admit there are still times, like this bout of whooping cough, that we are reminded of the gloomiest days of what we call our Spleen Year.

The antibiotics didn't seem to help much. Of course, we understood that only infants or people with suppressed immune systems are truly endangered by this illness. But the cough was wicked, and we lost, collectively, eighteen pounds over the course of the week. The house smelled. My wife was exhausted and couldn't keep up. Meals were too much of a chore, and for a stretch of thirty-five hours we ate nothing but applesauce and saltines. We drank ginger ale mixed with electrolyte-enriched water. Bored, we lay together in the living room—the couches and chairs and floors covered with old sheets, plastic-bagged trashcans by everyone's side—and watched television for hours on end, movie after movie. The Marx Brothers, Abbott and Costello, Martin and Lewis, our library of Disney and Pixar films, *I Love Lucy* and *Dick Van Dyke* marathons on Nickelodeon—slapstick stuff that delighted, though laughter was dangerous because it sometimes triggered a coughing fit in one of us, which inevitably spread to the rest, so that the house seemed to tremble. I couldn't help but picture patients in a tubercular ward spastically coughing blood into their bleached hankies.

After four days of antibiotics, the children slept through the night. The Health Department finally lifted the quarantine. Two days later, after the children were put to bed, my wife broke down and cried.

"At least it wasn't the spleen," I said, to cheer her.

During the Spleen Year, my wife and I didn't make love for eight months. Every moment not spent in worry or poring over medical research or care for our son and younger children had been devoted to sleep or upkeep or, somehow, work, though we did precious little of that, exhausting our sick leave and retirement accounts, mortgaging our house twice, selling both our cars and relying on a used one her mother lent us. Sex seemed then like a foreign, impossible act, something we remembered having done before but not with any clarity or sense of yearning. Bodies seemed to me angry, insolent saboteurs. Yet during that year we were as intimate as we had ever been or, I imagine, ever will be. We moved through the long months connected by frail but palpable spiritual threads, which I remember as a rare gift.

The night after the Whooping Cough Winter, as we dubbed it, was officially over, my wife and I made love with a rapturous, starved intensity that I couldn't remember experiencing in our many years together. Afterward, stunned and a little embarrassed, we held each other tightly.

My wife nodded off, but I felt restless. I remember thinking that we'd never really given ourselves over to the pure wonder of this kind of pleasure, the essential glorious urgency of sex. We'd been deprived—deprived ourselves—of this experience.

Or maybe we had experienced this before, and I'd just forgotten, the way a woman forgets the labors of childbirth. Or perhaps it only seemed this way because we'd just emerged from the trauma of this family sickness, and the juxtaposition of our vulnerability with the vitality of sex stunned and surprised.

I tried to close my eyes and meditate, hoping that by concentrating on nothingness, which I learned in a transcendental meditation class I'd taken during the Spleen Year, I would be carried off into sleep. But I only felt more restless. The anxiety that had temporarily dissipated seemed to come back, redoubled. I worried that perhaps this was the onset again of the insomnia that had knitted up the raveled sleeve of care, as my wife liked to say, for all those months during the Spleen Year—the insomnia that induced my migraines and sent me wandering the dispiriting streets of our small mountain town night after night.

It's not that bad, I told myself. *It's over.* But I couldn't will myself to sleep, even though the house was amazingly quiet, not a single cough or rustle. I marveled at the silence, and then rose, panicked, put on my robe, and checked the children to make sure they were breathing. I recognized in myself the same panic that seized me during the worst days of the Spleen Year. The panic that kept me awake, the fear that my children would die in their sleep, that fear prompting me obsessively to their rooms, not just to the sick one but to the well ones too, each hour, on the hour, to watch their chests rise and fall, rise and fall, until I was absolutely sure they would be fine, that they wouldn't stop breathing while I slept.

I went to the kitchen and scooped chocolate mint ice cream into a bowl and watched *Sports Center*, but it bored me. I surfed the channels until the senseless chatter of the talk shows and the infomercials and the late-night sitcom reruns in the otherwise silent house sounded to me like an obscenity. Exams I needed to grade for my first-year law students sat neglected in a rubber-banded folder on my desk in the corner of the living room. I wasn't about to start on those.

I opened the front door, stepped onto the porch, and sat in the swing. A warm night for March, and surprisingly dark with no moon, no clouds covering the stars, essentially no breeze. Without really thinking about it, I stood up, unbelted my robe and let it fall. Naked, I walked out to the end of the dark driveway, where I stood for several minutes just to feel the stillness of the night. It was a foolish act; I knew it then. Even now I'm not sure why I did it. But it felt good, I must admit, and eased some of my anxiety. It re-channeled the irritation.

I heard a coyote howl in the distance, and another one respond. The coyotes sometimes roam our neighborhood, and on occasion I'll hear them chasing some smaller animal, the mad yapping followed by the squeal of a rabbit, a cat, or perhaps a small dog.

The coyotes killed our dog, a dachshund-miniature collie mix. Another victim of the Spleen Year. My oldest son and my wife and I were scheduled to fly to Houston the next afternoon for the final, and what the surgeon warned us would be the most dangerous, of my son's surgeries. That night, we'd heard the yelping of the dog and then the frantic yapping of the coyotes. I went out with a flashlight and a baseball bat, and then shouted at them until, snarling, they ran away. I wore only my pajama bottoms and slippers, and clutching the smooth handle of the bat, I shined the light on the ground where the coyotes had been. The sight of the dog's chest and stomach turned inside out repulsed and fascinated me. I put the dog in a black plastic garbage bag (a detail that still makes me wince with shame) and buried him in the backyard before the kids awoke.

The next morning was one of the grimmest days in our family's history. My wife and the children and I sobbed for hours, something that had not happened with this kind of abandon or intensity through all the consultations and surgeries and chemo and radiation and incessant hand-wringing. I knew that what we were crying for was not our dog but all the worst fears we'd refused to voice—afraid that, by voicing those fears, we'd be transported to a reality that none of us wanted to imagine, as if talking about the worst might invoke it.

The killing of the dog seemed like a bad omen. We had become superstitious people. My wife talked weekly on the phone with a psychic in San Francisco. Her resorting to the psychic seemed like a desperate act, something I understood and tried to be respectful of, though it sometimes made me unaccountably angry and made me think less of my wife, though I knew that wasn't fair. Hadn't I talked to doctors and read medical journals and searched the internet for the most radical treatments and controversial procedures with the same desperation myself, and hadn't most of what I read only temporarily soothed my nightmares? We clutch for hope where we can, where our temperaments lead us. And none of us should have that yearning held against us.

Our son's tests were clear for three months, then six months, then a year, and gradually we felt safer, as if we were swimmers who'd gone too far out to sea in the middle of a storm, and after exhausted, seemingly futile efforts to swim back to shore, we could finally see the water foaming on the thin line of white beach.

I must admit that I sometimes find myself missing that time in our lives. I miss the realm of precariousness in which we lived. I would never tell my wife this. Even to write it here, though it is the truth, frightens me, makes my hand tremble, as if I might be inviting trouble.

There I was, outside at the end of my driveway, alone, without my clothes. I started walking down the street. Only after I was blocks away did I acknowledge to myself that, if someone spotted me, I might very well be arrested. But at that moment I didn't care, and on some level perhaps I wanted to be caught.

When I was a young lawyer, working as a public defender in Tucson, I never ceased to be amazed by the stupidity of my clients, the stunned and sometimes placid look on their faces when I would visit them in their cells, as if they didn't know how this had happened to them, or they did know how it happened but still seemed unwilling to admit that they'd brought the calamity upon themselves. After three years of those faces, I knew practical law was not for me and leapt at the first opportunity I could to teach, even if it meant a radical pay cut and teaching students whose faces sometimes reveal those same looks of imbecility and complicity.

At any rate, this naked walk in the dark was something new and strange for me. Not even during the Spleen Year, when I walked incessantly through town in the hours before sunrise (wearing out three pairs of expensive running shoes in six months), had I ever done something like this. Maybe I'd gone nuts. A side-effect of the medicine or the whooping cough itself. Or a delayed reaction—this relatively minor family illness the last straw, the one that would tip me over into madness.

For a while, I felt invulnerable on those dark, silent streets, until a woman opened a door and shouted, with the unmistakable viciousness provoked by too much alcohol, "Who's there?"

I darted into the shadows behind a hedge. I didn't answer, but I could hear my own panting breath.

"Gary? Wallace?" she called. "That you? You stay away from here, I mean it. I'm calling the police, you bastards!"

The door slammed shut, and after a moment I hoisted myself up and ran, avoiding the streetlamps, toward home. A car approached. The headlights forced me to dive flat on a lawn, bare ass to the moon, until it passed.

At my house, I robed myself and sat on the porch swing until my breathing returned to normal and the sweat cooled on my body. I was surprised I hadn't begun coughing again.

Once inside, I listened to the house. Except for the humming of the refrigerator, it was so quiet. I walked down the hall and checked on the girls, pulled the covers up over their skinny bodies, felt their foreheads to make sure they weren't feverish, kissed their cheeks. Then I checked the boys. My youngest son curled tightly under his blankets, his pillow covering half his face. I tucked the pillow under his head.

Then I turned to my oldest son. He lay on his back, arms outstretched, head tilted with his mouth open. His pajama top had crept up his chest, and I could see, in the glow of the Spiderman nightlight, the raised ridges of his surgery scars. I ran my fingers lightly along the edges, to feel their shape and texture. He turned over to his side, and I draped the sheet and blanket over him and kissed his cheek.

In my bedroom, my wife still slept. I ran my hand along the covers and then leaned over and kissed her lips, though she did not wake.

I still wasn't sleepy, not in the least. I could smell the pungency of my body, the grassy smell from my dive onto the lawn, and underneath it all the odor of sex from earlier. I needed a shower. In the bathroom, I turned on the lights and was surprised by the sight of myself, my face gaunt and flushed, my hair, flecked with silver, shooting out in a comic way. I hung my robe on the hook and examined myself—a middle-aged body, my skin too white, almost translucent, blue veins like tendrils beneath, my neck mottled, my torso thinned out by this week of illness. My ribs like splayed fingers beneath my flesh.

I started the water, and only when I reached below the sink to get a washcloth and a towel did I notice the blood. All over the bathroom floor. The adrenaline kicked in, thrilling and scaring me, and threatening, if I wasn't careful, to tip me into a migraine. This is how they always started. *Where did the blood come from where did it come from where did it come from?* jangled my body like an alarm.

I opened the bathroom door so that the light spilled into the bedroom. The hardwood was tracked with blood, as well as the rug by the end of the bed. I had kissed my wife, but did not think to look under the sheets or to check her breathing as I had checked my children's.

I looked down and saw that I was standing in it, the blood. I was confused. Only when I stepped back did I realize the blood was coming from *me*. From my *feet*.

I shut the door and sat on the closed toilet lid and lifted one foot and then the other to inspect my soles. The pads were scraped, a jagged cut on my left instep and over my toes, tiny pebbles embedded in the flesh. I felt no pain whatsoever. My feet looked like those of a stranger's. *Am I in shock?* I wondered. Must be. Or perhaps it was simply the adrenaline, which had been pumping all along. Maybe that's why I didn't feel the pain when I was out running through the neighborhood. Still, I was perplexed by this moment, divorced from the obvious pain, as if some switch had been turned off in my nerve endings, sparing me.

I unspooled toilet paper and gently swabbed the blood. I put the washcloth under the warm water, wrung it out, and began to clean my right foot and then my left. I reached in the drawer for tweezers and removed the small pebbles and grains of dirt lodged in the cuts, and then dabbed again. I sat on the side of the tub and placed my feet in the warm water to soak, watched the water turn red, the swirls quickly brightening into a beautiful pattern. It astonished me that this had happened, and that I had not really felt it. There wasn't even a dull ache. It seemed miraculous really, but I didn't know whether or not this was a good thing. Pain, I understood, was the way the body protected you, made you aware that you were indeed alive. I wondered if my body was protecting or betraying me.

Finally my feet began to throb, which gave me some modicum of relief, though I still felt vulnerable, amazed that this much damage could have happened unnoticed, or *ignored*, by me. I knew that the real pain would creep in soon enough. I knew that I'd be nursing these wounds for days or weeks, and that it would hurt to walk for some time to come. *Ridiculous*, I thought, *that I have—or had—such baby feet.*

I looked forward to telling my wife about it, making a joke, though I could already imagine her confusion, worry, and then her annoyance, her left eyebrow arched in skepticism, the small, exasperated shake of her head. She'd already been tending to us and was exhausted by it; she didn't need any more invalids.

What I mainly felt, at that moment, was a sense of amusement, a sense of pleasure at my own foolishness. I decided to dub this the Night of the Bloody Soles. It made me laugh, and it was the first time that I could remember feeling this kind of absurd gaiety in some time. It's not a bad thing to recognize your own foolishness and to be able to laugh at it. It proves that you are fundamentally sane.

I pulled my feet from the water and dried them, staining the towel in the process. I knew I should get some alcohol, antibiotic ointment, and gauze from the hall closet. I also knew that I should clean up the floors before my children and wife awoke. I didn't want them to be alarmed, seeing the bloody tracks by the sides of their beds.

But how to get from the bathroom to the hallway without making more of a mess?

I felt strangely disoriented. I stared down at my footprints on the bathroom floor. They were just a jumble, as if the man who did this was confused about where he was going or trying to learn a dance he didn't understand. That thought made me smile. I wiped away the footprints with the towel.

Then suddenly I felt very sleepy, as if I'd been injected with a tranquilizer—a droopy, narcotic wooziness. I could go to sleep right here in the bathroom. Just take a little nap, clear my head before dealing with the mess I'd made. I pulled another clean towel from beneath the sink and propped it under my head like a pillow. I reached up and turned off the light.

It wasn't completely dark. I wanted to just lie there—*in self-quarantine*, I told myself—and watch the way the bluish pre-dawn light filtered through the opaque bubble glass of the bathroom window. It was really quite beautiful. My bloody feet throbbed, but it wasn't painful yet, so I let myself enjoy that sweet territory between sleep and consciousness—the coolness of the wood, the soft, clean towel against my cheek, that blue light just on the other side of my eyelids—the heightened sensitivity to the world that happens after sickness or before the onset of expected suffering.

Orchestration

Ah yes the last seven now almost eight years full of all those babies and light and love but let's not get too misty-eyed that we forget the comic drudgery of our lives and in exchange for our small piece of immortality we get to labor for twenty-five years in the salt mines of full-throttle parenthood so I want to sing an unending song to these years and not just a light melodic "My Cup Runneth Over with Love" but also a hard-driving blues number with a too-loud drumbeat and a deep bass guitar and every once in a while the insistent whine of a saxophone or the shrill scream of a trumpet and I want to sing the rock and roll of sleepless nights and boulder breasts and leaking nipples and dark circles under our eyes and feel the rhythm guitar of spit-up rags and laundry piled everywhere and dishes stacking in the sink and layers of dust like sheep's wool on the furniture and I want to croon an ode to peanut butter and jelly sandwiches bean burritos macaroni and cheese fruit cocktail whole milk raisins sugary cereal and granola bars and yodel a refrain of thanks for sippy cups high chairs minivans car seats baby wipes and plastic spaghetti bibs and let us jive to Fred Flintstone faces and middle-of-the-night feedings and accidents in the bed and overflowing toilets and emptied boxes of tissues scattered on the floor and crayon marks on linoleum and white walls and let us do a Beach Boys number to splashing baths and shampooed hair and chattering teeth and naked baby sprints and in a deep baritone let us chant a dirge to diapers diapers diapers diapers and always more diapers one long never-ending bowel movement and let us both find a two-octave harmony for cracked knuckles and stringy hair for stretch marks and love handles for split ends and prickly beards and floppy stomachs and let us do one more chorus for unopened mail and naptime meltdowns and loose teeth and let us hold our breaths and listen again to the flutist's cries of sore throats and coughs and runny noses and glass-eyed lethargy and let us rumba to sibling injustice and pleading calls for Pooh and Piglet and Floppy Bunny and Raggedy Ann and let us kiss the bruises and bandage the cuts and clip the fingernails and trim the bangs and wipe away the tears as we negotiate a jazz riff to eyedroppers and antibiotics chewable vitamins and cough syrup and then later we can mambo to the rattle of the kids' popper and vacuum cleaner and the crash of buggies and the volume of their play rising like a wave of brass band crescendos while we're talking on the phone and at night let us feel the mournful wail of parental rage and cry to the guilt-riddled tunes of the pictures we did not take the well-balanced meals we did not prepare the fluoride drops we neglected to administer and more sadly for the baby we lost and the baby who fell from a grocery cart and the baby who would not eat for weeks and let us sing a plaintive folksong for the accusations and angry oaths uttered in exhaustion and then in our dreams let us also remember the melodies of love songs hummed to each other in midday but fading into a drowsy funk by eight-thirty and then in the morning let us march in time to the pistons of the plastic breast pump and the family of ants hunting for the sugary milk in our bed and let us jitterbug to the delight of our children's voices at the park and the way they tell jokes and write stories and boss each other around and talk and sing and shout just to be hearing the sound of their own voices and let us hum a lullaby to their love of books and their love of each other and the way their minds absorb the world and the way they look when asleep and then let us whisper a still gentler lullaby to the downy smell of their infant bodies and the way they nestle in the crook of our arms or on our chests or between our flesh in bed and let us finally sit spellbound before this symphony of frantic order and let us study this music until we know like conductors the movements and the full stops and the trills and the *allegro* of weary days and wearier nights and the *legato* of their bruised spirits needing you or me to hold them and the strings of caution and the insistent drums of work and the pianos of joy and the cymbals of sex that got us into this predicament in the first place and those oboes and clarinets of frustration and foolishness and the tubas of grief and guilt and the brassy blare of this house of laughter and this home of thick and chaotic love.

IV

Filament

When she was seventeen, Loretta discovered that she was pregnant with Blue Simpson's child, a shame really. Not because Tildon turned out to be a bad son. (In fact, he would do quite well, thirty-two years later, buying and operating a chain of successful southern fried chicken franchises.) It's just that Loretta's future seemed genuinely promising before this turn of events. She'd graduated high school as the valedictorian when she was sixteen. Granted, this was in Honey Grove, Texas, so there were not that many students, certainly not that many bright ones, but she had nonetheless impressed her teachers enough to skip a couple of grades, and then went off to college in Denton on a full scholarship to study journalism. In Denton, she met Blue, a strawberry-headed pipe fitter and apprentice welder from Bug Tussle who liked to two-step. At the beginning of her sophomore year, he took her dancing every night for three straight weeks. By the end of that time, Tildon was conceived. Blue and Loretta hastily married during a freakish October snowstorm, and she gave up her academic pursuits and, until after Blue's death, her dream of becoming a reporter.

Tildon arrived the following spring, followed by two miscarriages that left her depressed and wishing she could return to the promising trajectory of her old life. But then Melinda was born, and Tanya soon after. They'd moved to Charnelle in the Texas Panhandle, where they lived in a too-small, too-hot cinderblock house near the drive-in. On summer weekend nights, she and the kids and Blue would climb up to the flat, pebbly roof, set up folding chairs and a blanket and watch the double feature for free. Those nights—as the Panhandle dusk turned a velvety blue, as the kids fell asleep in their sleeping bags, as she and Blue sipped beers and she nestled in the crook of his arm with a blanket wrapped around them, and, on one occasion, they actually made love, quietly, thrillingly, during the final fifteen minutes of *Double Indemnity*—those nights were, Loretta would reflect much later, the best times of the marriage.

Blue worked at Charnelle Steel, and Loretta stayed home in the cramped house and cared for the children. She gradually realized, too late, that she had no special knack for mothering. It wasn't that she felt a particular animosity toward her children, but rather against motherhood itself. At first she was ashamed of this epiphany, but after a few years, she no longer tried to deny it. She didn't confess it to others, certainly not to Blue or the children. People tended to harbor a grudge against mothers who seemed to dislike their own, even though, from what she could tell, it was a common enough occurrence. To acknowledge her feelings, to herself at least, eased her conscience a little and rekindled the sense of disciplined observation and fidelity to truth, no matter how unpleasant, that had made her want to pursue a life in journalism. The effort to be kind and compassionate also demanded from her a rigorous testing of her spirit that was, she felt, not unlike prayer, even though she didn't consider herself a religious woman.

Loretta believed she would have adapted just fine to this situation if matters had not taken a turn for the worse in the eighth year of her marriage when a miniscule filament of hot steel wedged itself in Blue's left eye. The accident ironically had not taken place at work, so Charnelle Steel claimed no responsibility. Nearly blind in that eye, Blue returned, after surgery and a month and a half of recuperation, to work, but his disposition soured with the disfigurement, the now-endless medical bills, and the bad luck of getting an injury that, if he'd been more fortunate, could have resulted in a handsome settlement and perhaps a semi-comfortable life of early retirement.

Most mornings he left for work by five and didn't return until six-thirty or seven, later if he happened to stop off at the Armory for drinks and to shoot a little pool, at which he was deceptively skilled, despite his bad eye. When he arrived home on these nights to the house that never seemed to stay clean or uncluttered, the dust growing like moss on the furniture, he often felt the walls squeezing him, a claustrophobic bitterness puddling like acid in his stomach. His wife had grown too thin, with a hostile little smirk nestled in the corners of her mouth, though she wasn't even thirty yet. She'd always been smart, and perhaps that was the real problem. He'd wooed her away from college. He knew she held against him the life he'd provided for them. But that had been as much her fault as his, if fault was to be found. It seemed unjust the way her lips drew tight like a purse string, the way she seemed to hold him responsible for her regrets, without ever acknowledging that he was the one with the goddamn bad eye, who had to work seventy, sometimes eighty hours a week, relegated to the shitty welding jobs rather than the custom work he'd been trained and paid well to do, and still *could* do if just given half a chance. Entering the house, he often felt as if he'd been lit on fire, as if his whole body was a breeding ground for army ants, a feeling exacerbated by the holes in his shirt and little blisters and pockmarks beneath the holes where the torches had burned and re-burned his forearms and neck and wrists.

Loretta understood how his predicament might embitter him, but it didn't seem right that he'd sometimes take it out on her and the children, shouting for them to *shut up, shut up, just for holy chrissakes shut the fuck up,* and after the injury, occasionally and then more routinely striking Loretta, once even with his brown leather belt, the buckle of which left a puncture in her hip that had become infected and never completely healed. A blistered scab chafed under the elastic waistband of her slip.

After these incidents, he would leave, setting out for the Armory or, in lonelier moods, on long drives to the nearby lakes or to the Waskalanti Creek where he'd get out, take off his shoes and socks, cuff his jeans and wade into the cold running water, the smooth pebbles caressing his feet. He'd wait for the train to roll across the wooden bridge at five minutes past midnight. Pressing his hands against the posts when the train passed, he would feel the trestle shake and the surprising heat shimmy to the bottom of the foundation. Standing in the cold water and touching those warm vibrating wooden posts soothed him.

After he returned, calmer, contrite even, he'd sometimes take his guitar from the closet, wake the children and sing to them, ballads he'd learned before he was married, when he dreamed of traveling with a band from dancehall to dancehall all the way to Nashville. Tildon, Melinda, and Tanya warily appreciated this part of the evening and came to recognize it as a prelude to quieter months before their father's dangerous sap would rise again.

Later in bed with Loretta, he'd stroke her stomach as he kissed the places where he'd bruised her, and then he'd make love to her with a tenderness that she relished, even if she didn't like the road by which they'd arrived at this place, nor did she want any more children, and had taken to cleansing herself afterward, once Blue'd fallen asleep, with a foul-smelling potion that she purchased from Maria Fernandez, the midwife who lived in what was back then called Mexican Town on the east side of Charnelle.

The next morning she would stir into a cup of hot tea a yellow powder, also provided by Maria Fernandez, that tasted like formaldehyde smelled. Then she'd spend the rest of the day in the bathroom vomiting and sometimes spotting, even if it wasn't her time of the month. It seemed to her a heavy price to pay for an hour of tenderness, but she did not want to imagine another child in this house.

On March 22nd of the twelfth year of their marriage, Blue came home late with more burn holes in his shirt than normal. He'd been to the Armory where he'd drunk six shots of tequila and lost twenty-eight dollars on a double-or-nothing rack of Nine Ball. When he arrived, at nearly midnight, he struck Loretta twice across the face, and then drove to the Waskalanti Creek and stood under the trestle in the ice cold water, waiting, but the train never came. He'd missed it. After a while, he felt soothed just the same by the hooting of the owls, out now for spring, and the purr of the tequila in his body, which rendered him, as it often did, feeling more alert than sleepy, though he knew even in his drunkenness that he might not remember a damn thing the next day. He drove home and woke the children, who patiently listened to him strum a song he'd written himself years ago called "Long Train Rolling" followed by a particularly soulful rendition of "Blue Moon of Kentucky," and then he kissed them and carried Tanya to bed, nearly toppling over the nightstand in the children's room.

"I love you," he said and lingered by the door.

After a long pause, Melinda said, "I love you, too, Daddy," though Tildon remained quiet, feigning sleep. Tildon knew what his father wanted, but he could not bring himself to appease the man's wish to be forgiven.

Blue shut his bedroom door, shed his clothes into a puddle, and stretched out over his wife and began to kiss her. She pushed him away.

"I'm sorry, honey, I'm so sorry," he said and then wept for a good ten minutes. "I'm a sorry bastard, I know. Sorry sorry sorry."

She remained unmoved. He pried her knees open, cooing into her ear. She felt and then, surprising even herself, acted upon an impulse to claw his back and his face. He cuffed her clumsily across the temple, but she didn't make a sound. He held her arms down, and they wrestled on the bed until Tildon knocked on the door, tentatively whispering, "Is everything all right?"

Tildon's words provoked a momentary truce, both of them unsure what to do next. Blue said, "Get on back to bed, son."

"Mom?" Tildon said, and Loretta heard, alongside her son's fear, his desire to help her. *Please,* he seemed to be telling her, *please please tell me what I should do,* and *please don't have me do a thing.* That voice broke her heart.

"Mind your father," she said as lightly as she could.

They heard him retreat, and then, without resistance, she let Blue finish what he'd started, holding the headboard so that it wouldn't thump against the wall and alarm the children any more than they were already alarmed. It was over in a matter of minutes. She pushed him off her. He rolled over and fell asleep.

She opened the door. Tildon and Melinda sat huddled in their pajamas outside, their backs against the wall.

"Everything's okay," she said. "Go on to bed." They didn't move at first, but then she said, "Hurry up, now. It's late." Her voiced pacified them, and they obeyed.

She went to the bathroom, where she cleaned herself and doctored her face, and then returned quietly to the children's room to make sure they were asleep. The girls were both out, but Tildon was merely pretending. She didn't question him, though, just kissed all their foreheads. She whispered in his ear, "Don't you worry." And then she left the room, closing the door behind her.

She started to go back to her bedroom, but couldn't bring herself to do it. She shuffled into the dark living room and lay on the sofa, where she just wanted to close her eyes for a few minutes and collect herself. The house was silent except for the whisper of branches brushing against the window. She rose and went to the kitchen, where she thought about administering Maria Fernandez's remedies. She knew that she would begin vomiting in an hour or so if she did, so she decided to wait. After pulling her favorite cast iron skillet from the cabinet, she shifted it from hand to hand, feeling its familiar heaviness. She drank a glass of water slowly, rinsed the glass, put it in the drainer, and then carried the skillet back to the bedroom.

She shut the door and pulled the cord on the lamp so that a yellow glow enveloped the bed, where her husband lay, his mouth agape, his naked body sprawled over the tangled sheets. He looked like a dead man, limp and pale, splotched with blisters at his neck and wrists. Holding the cool and slightly greasy handle, she raised the skillet and hit him across his face, the flat bottom covering his nose and right eye socket. She heard bone crack and felt his blood spray her arm and the hollow of her throat.

Immediately, she knew that she hadn't hit him as hard as she had wanted to. She had wanted to crush his skull, and she felt she would have been justified in doing so, but at the last second she'd held back just enough so that only his nose and perhaps his cheek appeared to break. He did not move, though, and she was unsure whether or not she had, despite her failure of courage, killed him.

For a solid sixty seconds, she watched him, counting each second. He still didn't move. She sat down on the chair next to the bed with the skillet in her lap.

Tentatively, she put her hand on his chest, searched for the *thump-thump* of his heartbeat. She tipped his chin away from her and inspected the broken part of his face. His nose and cheekbone were starting to swell and appear pulpy. The dried blood from the earlier scratches created a black line running from his temple to his jaw, another one on his forehead. Fresh blood from his nose trickled over his upper lip. The sheets were flecked with blood. She reached over to the dresser and pulled a clean handkerchief from the top drawer and dabbed gently at his face until the white cotton turned red.

When he woke forty minutes later, she was holding a cloth full of ice against his nose and cheek. Groggily, still in shock, he asked, "What happened?"

"The dresser tipped over onto the bed. We're lucky it didn't kill us both."

She could tell he didn't believe her. In all this time of waiting, she hadn't given one thought to what she would say when he woke. She was surprised by the words that came out of her mouth. It seemed outlandish even to her, but she decided, out of curiosity, to leave it at that, to offer nothing else in order to see how he'd respond. She was even more surprised that he didn't challenge her story, just lay there, limp and swelling. He pulled the sheet up over his exposed body.

When he said nothing, she felt some crucial element of power in her marriage shift.

At five-thirty, he went to work with his nose bandaged, the cuts on his face beginning to harden, his good eye as threaded with broken blood vessels as his bad one had been several years before.

When Tildon and the girls woke, shortly after their father left, they studied their mother's face, but she understood that they didn't really want her to tell them anything. The inner life of a marriage must be kept hidden from children. She knew that much. Loretta made them oatmeal and toast, fixed their lunches, and hurried them off to the bus stop, and then she bathed quickly. She remembered that she hadn't taken Maria Fernandez's powder. Maybe it wouldn't make her vomit this time. Maybe she had built up immunity, like a person who is bitten several times by snakes becomes snake-proof. But when she went to the pantry and opened the tin can on the top shelf where she kept the powder hidden, she found it empty. She would deal with that later. Right now, she needed to remain as clear-headed as possible. She put on her nicest wool skirt and dark purple sweater and walked down to the courthouse.

"I want a divorce," she told the clerk, Gail Weathers, a man who'd lost all four fingers of his left hand in the war.

"Why?" he asked.

"I don't love my husband anymore."

"That ain't a good enough reason for the state of Texas."

She pointed to her bruised face, and when he still seemed unconvinced, she discreetly rolled back the waistband of her skirt and slip to reveal the belt buckle puncture, a halo of swollen pink flesh surrounding the still-infected hole. This got Weathers' attention, mainly because of the audacity of the revelation rather than the impressiveness of the wound. But he didn't show his surprise, just continued chewing on an already-gnawed toothpick.

"Guess you should talk to Hef Givens," he said.

She walked over to the office of Hef Givens, one of only two lawyers in town.

"A divorce'll cost you more than it's worth," he said. "And you can be sure Blue won't take it well."

Hef Givens and Blue Simpson sometimes hunted deer together. He was not excited about being enlisted as the attorney in a divorce proceeding against his friend.

"Here," Loretta said, handing Hef Givens twenty-five dollars for his retainer, money she had been hoarding the past year by shaving a couple of dollars off the grocery bill each month. "That's all I have right now."

These were not, despite post-war prosperity, exactly fat times in Charnelle, but Hef Givens was doing well enough. He did not need to take on this case. But his own father had been a thief who sometimes savagely beat his mother and him, and then deservedly spent seven years in jail for armed robbery—a time of poverty for Hef and his mother, yet also a period of relative safety and occasional happiness, especially after they moved to Charnelle to live with his grandparents.

Hef looked at Loretta, an intelligent but sullen woman, and saw in her bruises and resolve a refracted portrait of his own mother's life. "Okay, then," he said, without touching the money. "Here's the first order of business."

She returned home, as Hef Givens instructed her to do, and packed Blue's personal belongings into two boxes, which she placed on the porch, along with a suitcase filled with his clothes. She took the children to Carol Lippincott's house. Then she called the sheriff and requested that a deputy be sent to escort Blue away when he arrived home.

The sheriff's office had already received a call from Hef Givens, and no one there relished this assignment. They didn't appreciate domestic situations, since those were often the only dangerous ones in Charnelle. Not many people were injured with criminal intent in the county unless, experience had taught Sheriff Britwork, they were on the receiving end of a love gone sour. In 1949, there was very little by way of criminal activity at all in Charnelle, so Sheriff Britwork and his four officers spent most of their time at the Ding Dong Daddy Diner, drinking coffee and munching onion rings, or hanging out at the high school football and basketball games to prevent adolescent brawls, or cruising through Mexican Town to make sure the residents knew that someone was keeping a suspicious eye on them. There were also no divorces recorded in Charnelle during the previous six years, even if a majority of marriages, by Britwork's estimation, were not happy ones. Sometimes a couple would separate temporarily, or a man would run off with a mistress for a while, or a wife would run off with her husband's best friend, only to return a few days or weeks later. These incidents seldom resulted in divorce. Acrimony, certainly, and a malignant resentment. Sometimes shots were fired or knives wielded or suicides threatened. But seldom divorce.

The sheriff sent Fortney Nevers, the pudgy twenty-year-old deputy, out to the Simpson home to oversee the proceedings. This wasn't a kind assignment on the part of the sheriff, but Britwork had a root canal performed that very morning—the fourth of what would eventually be six surgeries—and he was not in a generous mood. He didn't want to be the one dealing with a marital dispute, especially between Blue and Loretta Simpson. He had known them since they first moved to Charnelle. The sheriff and his wife had even played pinochle with the Simpsons a time or two before both couples were besieged by children. Britwork would now and again shoot a game of pool with Blue at the Armory, but since Blue's accident a few years ago, the two families seldom saw each other, and that was just fine with the sheriff. Blue Simpson carried his misfortune and self-pity around like a virus, and the sheriff didn't want to catch it.

Besides, it would serve Fortney Nevers right. The young deputy annoyed the sheriff. The boy's fatness was particularly galling to Britwork, a man with the metabolism of a greyhound, who harbored an unreasonable prejudice against the portly.

"Nevers ain't old enough," Britwork once told his other officers, within earshot of the deputy, "to have earned the right to be fat."

The sheriff had been forced to hire the twenty-year-old because Fortney's uncle was the Honorable Cleavis Nevers, the county judge. Given the irritable mood the root canal had fostered in Britwork, he half-hoped that Blue Simpson might beat the shit out of the young deputy—not badly enough to inflict serious injury, of course, but enough to persuade the pudgy kid to give up on police work.

Months later, at Fortney Nevers' trial, the sheriff would change his tune. He would testify that the deputy was a model policeman, and that he was confident Fortney could handle the assignment when he sent him to the Simpsons' house that day. The sheriff would tell the court that he was sure the boy had warned Blue Simpson not to take another step, and that he had fired the shot only to scare the man. The jury would acquit Fortney Nevers, in large part because of their fondness for Hef Givens, who had agreed to represent the young officer, and out of deference to Judge Nevers, who reluctantly recused himself from the case but sat on the front row, directly behind his nephew, and stared solemnly at the jury members, as if issuing his own verdict. Sheriff Britwork would emerge as the incompetent one, the person in fact most culpable for the tragedy, a courtroom performance that would result in the loss of his job in the next election.

Fortney arrived at the Simpson home shortly before five-thirty. Two boxes and a suitcase were sitting ominously on the front porch, and Fortney wished he'd urinated before he left the station because he didn't want to be stuck inside the Simpson bathroom with his penis in his hand when Mr. Simpson showed up to what would most likely be an unpleasant situation. Fortney worried about wetting his pants while he was supposed to be officially presiding over a civil separation. He'd inherited a weak bladder from his father's side of the family, complicated by a serious kidney infection when he was a boy, and consequently he had to piss eight to ten times a day and often twice during the night. When he was nervous, he sometimes lost continence, which was not advantageous for a young man, especially a deputy—a predicament that forced him to order double-padded underwear from Montgomery Ward. This solution minimized but did not entirely eliminate his worry and shame.

Blue was already in a surly mood when he left for home. His eye itched and watered. His nostrils had swollen shut during the day, forcing him to breathe through his mouth, and now his throat was raw. He'd gobbled down aspirin every two hours to diminish the pain of his swollen nose and cheek and the scratches on his face and back, but it didn't seem to help much. To make matters worse, he'd had to field the same questions a dozen times from his co-workers about how his face had become mangled.

He repeated what Loretta had told him—that the dresser had fallen on him while sleeping. It had knocked him out and broken his nose, maybe busted his cheek. His co-workers' arched eyebrows and smirks reinforced the suspicion he'd already had that such an accident was unlikely at best and preposterous at worst. Moreover, he didn't have a good excuse for the scratches on his face, not to mention the unseen ones on his back and shoulders, and couldn't come up with any better story. He didn't tell them he'd gone a little nuts himself last night, drunk too much tequila, lost too much shooting pool, and did what he always regretted doing when he drank more than three shots and lost more than twenty dollars. Nor did he tell them that he didn't really remember much after that, except that he woke in the morning with his face swollen and aching, his nose broken, his eyes black.

"That dresser must've had some pretty sharp fingernails," Zeeke Tate said. The other men snickered in such a way that Blue understood he'd been and would continue to be the butt of jokes for days, maybe weeks, to come. It didn't help that, at four o'clock that afternoon, lightheaded and then dizzy, hyperventilating, he'd collapsed on the floor of the shop and had been forced to breathe into a paper bag that Bean Peterson, the foreman, put over his mouth.

How could the day be any more miserable? But then he arrived home to find a police cruiser parked on the curb, two boxes and a suitcase on the front porch, the door locked.

Blue rapped on the door, but no one answered. He didn't have his key. They never locked the house, except when they went for Christmas every other year to Bug Tussle and Honey Grove. He knocked again and heard footsteps on the other side, but no one answered.

"Open the damn door," he said.

"Take your things and leave," Loretta answered.

He pressed his cheek, the one that was not bruised, against the door, and could hear his wife breathing on the other side, her face just inches of wood from his.

"Open it!"

"No."

"I don't mind breaking this fucking door down." He said this flatly, without malice, which was a kind of victory, though he regretted the profanity. He didn't usually swear at his wife unless he'd drunk too much tequila, and he'd sworn off tequila soon after he'd become lightheaded today and found himself on the floor with a paper sack over his face.

The deadbolt was thrown. He waited a few seconds, and then opened the door to find Loretta standing on the other side of the room, near the fireplace.

"What are you doing?" he asked.

"Stay there," she said. There wasn't any alarm in her voice. In fact, he wondered if this might be an elaborate joke.

His sinuses throbbed, and he felt again the wooziness he'd experienced just moments before he'd passed out earlier in the day. He touched his nose. It felt tender and swollen—and he imagined that it was already turning a darker shade of purple. Both his good and bad eye began to itch and water, but he knew enough not to scratch that itch. It would only make things worse. He blinked a few times to clear his vision. A chubby boy in a uniform suddenly emerged from the bathroom.

"Who are you?" Blue asked.

"Deputy Nevers?" the boy said, his voice going up at the end so that his answer sounded like a question.

"You related to Judge Nevers?"

"I'm his nephew," Fortney said, almost embarrassed.

"Get out," Loretta said. "This officer will follow you to the Charnelle Inn or wherever you want to go. But you *must* leave. Now."

"What're you talking about?" Though Blue assumed that whatever he'd done last night could not have been good, given the state of his own face and hers, he didn't expect such immediate nor dire consequences for his actions. He just wanted, for now, to lie down in his own bed and sleep for about twelve hours.

"Blue. Now."

"Where're the kids?"

"Out," she said. Blue wasn't sure if she was referring to the children or issuing him another order. He breathed deeply through his mouth, having forgotten again, in the confusion of the moment, that this was the only way he *could* breathe. Dizziness seemed ready to engulf him.

"Come with me, Mr. Simpson," Fortney said nervously. "I'll help you load your things."

"Loretta," Blue said. He could hear a whine in his own voice, which surprised and embarrassed him.

"Go, Blue," she said, quieter now. He detected a trace of pity, a tenderness that he thought he might leverage to his advantage.

"Let's just you and me have a glass of tea and talk about it." He sat down in the chair closest to the door.

"No, Blue. You have to go."

"I don't feel so good, you know. It's been a hard day, Loretta. I need to rest."

"Sir," Fortney said, "I'm afraid you have to leave. I'll help you."

"You'll be hearing from Hef Givens in the morning," Loretta said.

"Hef Givens?"

"My lawyer."

"Hef? What do you mean Hef Givens is your lawyer? Hef is *my friend*."

He remembered suddenly, vividly, the last time he and Hef had gone hunting, both of them squatting in the bushes, the predawn light shrouding them, their breaths misting in the November air, both of them waiting, waiting, waiting for the bucks to appear on the meadow by the lake. He loved such moments, rare though they were, when he and another man, who also understood the dignity and beauty and suspense of such stillness, crouched together, watching and waiting patiently.

"It's over," she said.

"Come along, sir," the deputy said, his voice rising again in a way that reminded Blue of Tildon. *Where was Tildon? Where were the girls?*

Fortney put his hand on Blue's arm, a place where Blue had blistered himself that very day when he dropped the torch as he fell to the concrete floor. Blue knocked the boy's hand aside and stood up.

"Mr. Simpson," Fortney said, unsnapping the button on his holster. Fortney saw Blue glance down at the front of his pants. A small dark circle growing wider and wider. The man's swollen lips seemed to curl with the dismissive contempt Fortney had already put up with his whole damn life. Blue shoved him aside and took two long strides toward his wife.

Fortney would later swear under oath that he didn't aim for the man's back but for the fireplace, though after the trial he would sometimes remember or, in a feverish night sweat, dream it differently, would see his revolver pointed at a spot just below Blue Simpson's left shoulder blade, would feel again his finger squeezing the slightly oily steel of the trigger.

It was now dusk, and the lights were not yet on in the house. Loretta was surprised when her husband moved toward her, suddenly blocking the window. The shadowy outline of him reminded her of the young man—not even twenty, with a thin fuzz of reddish blond scruff on his chin and jaw—who had charmed her when she was at college in Denton. The night they'd met, Blue was standing on the edge of the dance floor. He'd offered his hand. She'd taken it, and he twirled her quickly through a double-time waltz, and she'd smiled, thanked him for the dance and started away, but then the next song began—a slow melancholy number, evocative, lovely—and he'd pulled her close, held her against him, and they'd moved in slow, swaying circles, and then he'd kissed her on the lips, a feather touch.

As he closed in on her now, she saw, in that split-second, his face clearly. His left eye disfigured. She almost thought she could see the filament of steel lodged there—like a tiny jagged flower. There it was, and then gone. She heard the sound of the shot, which echoed in the small room and kept ringing in her ears days later. Then she no longer saw Blue's features, just his distinct silhouette falling toward her, eclipsing the fading sun.

Relative Peace

When I found out what happened to Gene, I was flipping the ribs in the barbecue pit that my father welded for the restaurant, the heavy iron lid propped open with a crowbar, the heat rising steadily over the meat, so hot the air rippled in front of my eyes like a flag. The mesquite underneath the crusted grate splintered into red and orange before shrinking into white ash. It was five in the morning, and I'd been at work for nearly two hours, cutting and cooking the ribs and beef and pork, mixing coleslaw, molding hamburger patties. Most days during the week, I come in at five. But Saturdays get busy because the restaurant is located in the Westgate Mall. On these mornings I have to get a head start on the extra supply of barbecue for the day. Besides, I like the early-morning silence. Saev, the middle-aged Vietnamese man who prepares the batter and seasons the steaks and patties for me, doesn't usually arrive until eight, so I work several hours alone. I love the solitude, love the ritual of preparation before the cooks and waitresses arrive, before the hectic and sometimes maddening frenzy of the day: the lunch and dinner runs, the last-minute catering trips, the small kitchen tragedies, and my own temper.

I like this time to focus. In my life before this one, I rarely felt a moment's peace. What I've come to love, what I always really loved, was the simple rhythms of work. For the past eight years, ever since the fire, I'd been a new person: new marriage, a new start with this restaurant. I felt I'd been delivered, somehow, into a new life, and that life demanded the silence and peace of these mornings.

It'd been raining all through the night, a late autumn storm. Hail thumped against the roof. Wind whimpered down the vent chutes. Flipping the last side of ribs, I heard the back door open. I turned my head from the pit and rubbed the heat tears from my eyes with my sleeve. Cheryl, my wife, and Rich, my youngest brother, stood in the doorway, drenched. Cheryl wore her yellow slicker, her hood off. Water ran down her coat in thin rivulets. Rich wore a light blue coat with our Steak 'n' Taters logo over the heart, dark in patches because of the rain. His normally bushy hair clung to his head in dripping ringlets.

I was surprised to see Cheryl here—she hates getting up in the dark and had never been to the restaurant this early in the morning—but it was more of a shock to see Rich standing beside her. Rich had worked for me the last four and a half years as my floor manager and had quit only a month ago. It'd been coming for a while. But the final argument flared over something inane. I came in one afternoon to find him mixing a large tub of potato salad for a catering job. He'd poured in twice the amount of mustard and paprika, and the blob of potatoes was obviously ruined, a sickly yellow-red paste.

It seems stupid now, but a ruined tub of potato salad is like flushing money down the toilet. The argument led to shouting, chest pokes. He swung for my head and missed. I shoved him against the serving line, clutched his throat until the veins in his forehead pulsed, and then he kneed me in the groin, and I fell to the tile. He slung a huge metal meat pan that shattered a tray of tea glasses and tumbled across the serving line. And then he was gone, the door slamming behind him.

I hadn't seen or heard from him since. Despite the nastiness of our last fight, I wasn't upset about him being here now. When I hired Rich, he'd just gotten out of prison after serving seven months of an eighteen-month term for assault and kidnapping, which sounds worse than it was. He and his wife, Babs, had separated. Still somewhat delusional from a heat stroke he'd suffered on an offshore drilling rig in the Gulf of Mexico, Rich had driven all night to Amarillo to convince her to come back to him. When she refused, he tied her up, put her in the back of his pick-up, and headed to Houston. The manager of the apartment building called the cops, and within a few miles, they caught him. Babs was furious at first, but after she heard the circumstances of his offshore sickness, she was willing to forgive him. The district attorney was not so inclined, and Rich wound up in an El Paso prison until they let him out for good behavior.

Rich had been a sweet, funny kid, probably the most carefree of the five of us. But a series of car accidents, the divorce from Babs, and the prison time had transformed him into a sullen man with a chip on his shoulder. Granted, he was a good worker, dependable, fast, loyal to a fault. But what began as gratitude for the opportunity that I'd given him had turned, over the last year, into a growing resentment on both our parts. I felt somehow guilty with Rich around, just as sometimes

I felt guilty around my other siblings. My success had created an unspoken division among us. I was the lucky one. When Rich left, I felt secretly relieved not to have him here anymore. And perhaps he felt the same way.

So whatever this was about, I knew it was serious. Rich and Cheryl looked stricken. They stood at the door, not wanting to move any closer, as if a magic circle enclosed me, as if the water dripping from their clothes and the waves of heat from the pit prevented them from stepping inside.

I realized I still had a rib on the end of the long fork. I set it down, unhinged the crowbar, and closed the heavy lid. "What is it?"

"Bad news," Rich said.

"What's wrong?"

"It's Gene." Gene, the middle brother, four years younger than me and three years older than Rich. I hadn't seen him since Christmas, and then only briefly. He was not in good shape then, and I felt, before they could say a word, a chilling sense of certainty. I felt that, on some level, I had been waiting for this news—we all had been waiting for it—for a long time.

"Tell me," I said.

Rain splattered the roof, echoed down the vent chutes.

Rich looked at his feet. "Gene shot himself," he said, then stared coldly at me. "Right through his fucking heart."

Over the next three sleepless days and nights, Rich, Cheryl, and I took care of the arrangements. We identified the body, made calls, chose the coffin and headstone, shuttled to and from the airport and bus station to retrieve friends and relatives, explained again and again, as patiently as we could, the basic facts as we knew them.

Gene met his ex-wife, Gayle, at The Texas Moon, a dancehall on the eastern edge of Amarillo. They had argued, and then Gene grew angry and desperate. Gayle made a pretense of going to the restroom, then called the police and asked them to meet her at her house. Gene belligerently followed her in his truck. Seeing the squad cars at the house, Gene shut the engine off, then shot himself through the heart with a Colt .45 that had been our father's. He was rushed to the Baptist Hospital but died on the way.

By about the fifth time I told the story, I began to wonder if I'd subtly transformed Gene's death into a cry-in-your-beer ballad, a song to be accompanied by a steel guitar and whining fiddle, a simple refrain about the lonely, lovesick melancholy of the contemporary redneck. There was, I had to admit, something too white trash and pathetic about the whole episode. The newspaper story (accompanied by an old photo of Gene, thickly mustached, wearing his felt cowboy hat tipped back on his close-cropped head, smiling broadly), seemed to trivialize his life: "Local Cowboy Shoots Himself While Police and Ex-Wife Look On."

Some part of me admired the low-rent poetry of the newspaper story. I wanted the event to be this simple and manageable. I wanted, even then, to put Gene's death into perspective, to stake my words around it, cage it for myself so that it would make sense, would shrink into fact, into something static and confined and safe. But the more I tried to do this, the more I lowered my voice for his friends and our relatives and spoke with gravity, the more dishonest I felt, like an impostor. Gene felt more alive than ever to me, moving like a sly and dangerous animal among us.

The night before the funeral I went, alone, to see his body. It was the first time I'd been to a funeral home since my father died. The low lighting, the earnest still-life paintings, the dark wood furniture, and the nondescript instrumental music all seemed carefully designed not to offend anyone.

I hadn't seen Gene since the identification at the morgue, and I hadn't lasted very long there. I figured Rich would be the one to break down, since he's the youngest and had been closest to Gene, but it was me who left the room, nauseated and embarrassed. On the coroner's table, Gene looked like he would wake any second. His face had not completely lost its ruddy color, and his hair, which was longer than he usually kept it, was messed up, a cowlick curling in front like a red fishhook. There was a small, almost indefinable dab of purple, like plum jelly, staining the sheet, right over his heart. His lips were traced in faint blue, the same tint, I thought, of Cheryl's eyeshadow. That's when I lost it.

In the funeral casket, though, he looked more like a replica of himself in a wax museum. From the apartment where Gene had been staying, Rich retrieved a pair of good pants and Gene's favorite burnt-orange mohair vest. His black cowboy hat covered his hands and stomach. If you had met Gene only once or twice, you might think it was him. But of course it wasn't. I know that's what everyone says about seeing a body at a funeral home. But it's a fact. Morticians, God love them, just can't perform miracles, but I wanted them to at least get some basic things right. Gene's hair was too neat and parted on the wrong side. His cheeks seemed bloated, and the white pallor floated over his face like milk. I have never seen Gene that pale, not even in the morgue. I re-parted his hair with my comb and then walked to the front desk.

"My brother looks like a bloated fish," I told the undertaker, who listened patiently and then reset the lighting on the casket, putting more amber on Gene, so that his natural color seemed partially restored. He still didn't look right. I sat on the sofa where I could see only the edge of his face and the cowboy hat, and the distance allowed for the illusion that my brother was there, not alive but at least more of a familiar presence. If Gene had died any other way—if he'd stepped on a landmine in a war, or been stabbed in a barroom brawl, or crashed his truck on the highway, or contracted a fatal disease—then I might have fallen, as I wanted to, into a warm pool of nostalgia and pity. But his body and the way that he'd died seemed like an accusation.

There was good reason for me to feel accused. When I bought the Fina station in Charnelle, the small Texas Panhandle town where we grew up, and then brought Gene on as a partner, we fought all the time. And I'm not talking about simple shoving or wrestling matches. We were sometimes on the edge of murder. That was the nature of the relationship between all of us brothers. Once Gene attacked me with a crescent wrench and bashed my head enough times to require twelve stitches. I still have the scar.

These outbursts of violence occurred every couple of years, a result of working eighty- and hundred-hour weeks together. But, strangely enough, that wasn't the worst part. What goaded me, day-to-day, was Gene's irresponsibility with money. Over the years, particularly after our time at the Fina station, when he worked for the railroad, Gene wrote hot checks and explained to the unsuspecting recipients that if there were any problems, I'd clear things up. He disappeared for months at a time, and his debtors showed up at the restaurant ready to make a scene, to ruin my credit if I did not make good on my brother's promises.

He was a hard enough worker when he was around, but I'd fired him too many times to count, and we finally agreed, just a year and a half before his death, that we would no longer mix business with family. Since then, we hadn't communicated much. I didn't go see him in the rehab center where he committed himself for two weeks after he broke up with Gayle and started drinking heavily again. Frankly, I was fed up and didn't take it that seriously. He had to dry out, get his bearings straight after a break-up. He'd been through the same routine when he and his first wife, Angie, split up. Why worry?

It sounds callous, I imagine, but I'm a practical man. It was the Christmas season, the busiest time of year for me, when the calendar fills with holiday banquets and catering jobs, and the restaurant is on a wait-list all day long. I'd been too busy, and when Gene was released from rehab, he dropped by for fifteen minutes to say hello. He told me a joke about three whores, a rodeo clown, and a one-eyed bull. I fed him a barbecue sandwich, and he left. I knew he wasn't doing great, but he seemed fine enough not to worry too much.

As I sat in the funeral parlor—his body a few paces away, the silence of the blue room eerie—I wondered what I might have done to prevent this. Then I said to hell with these thoughts. They get you nowhere. I stood up, my legs and back stiff from sitting so long in one position, and walked over to the body. I stared at that face, no longer the face of my brother, just a mask. But Gene's presence was suddenly everywhere. I wished I could muster up some coherent emotion, but I just felt numb. I patted his chest and started out the door.

Gayle was in the lobby. I hadn't seen her yet, only talked to her briefly on the phone when I promised to take care of the funeral arrangements and expenses.

"Are you leaving?" she asked.

"On my way out."

Gayle is plain-looking—short, flat-chested, with coarse, straight hair. When she laughs, she does so unexpectedly, startlingly, so that it sounds like a shriek. She's smart enough, but she didn't finish high school. She got pregnant and divorced before she was out of her teens. Maybe that's what made her cynical about her lot in life and about men. Rich loathed her, and his version of the story went something like this: She was a hard, cruel bitch—unfair and manipulative. She took advantage of Gene's vulnerabilities, played upon his quick temper and pride, tugged him around like he was a stupid steer with a nose ring.

I could see the clarity and necessity of this story for Rich; I understood how he believed that Gene's suicide stemmed directly from his troubled relationship with this woman. But I didn't even remotely feel this way, even if I could understand Rich's point of view. I liked Gayle, always had. I never told anyone, but when Gene married her, I secretly felt my brother had been lucky to find her, to have a woman who matched, or at least balanced, his carelessness, his anger, his reckless qualities. The family had loved his first wife, Angie, as if she was one of our own, even siding with her when she and Gene broke up. But I admired Gayle more. When Gene and Gayle divorced, I was disappointed, not so much for Gene's sake, but for my own. She was no longer family and thus no longer a necessary, or even permissible, part of my life.

In the funeral home lobby, she started to remove her wet coat, and I helped her with it. "Are you doing okay?" I asked.

"I reckon."

She moved closer, and it occurred to me that she wanted to be hugged but was unwilling to initiate the action. This made me nervous.

"I have to go," I said. "I've been here nearly two hours already."

"Could you stay a little longer?" she asked. "I don't want to be alone with him."

We went back into the room with the casket, and I retreated to the sofa while she stood over the body.

"I fixed his part and had the man change the light," I said. "He looked awful with the lighting they had on him. Like a . . . ." I trailed off.

She didn't say anything. I tried not to watch her, but I couldn't help myself. She wore black, tight-fitting slacks, low-heeled shoes, and a simple navy blue blouse. Her hair was long and loose around her shoulders. It was clear she hadn't slept much either. Dark shadows under her eyes, her forehead wrinkled with worry lines as she stared at the body. There was a ravaged beauty about her that had always fascinated me, as if she lived in a realm of sensual chaos that I had worked my whole life to avoid but that riveted my attention nonetheless. She stood there for the longest time, in a trance almost, fiddling with Gene's hands and hair and mustache.

She mumbled something I couldn't hear. Then she said, very distinctly, "You son of a bitch."

I got up and put my arm around her shoulder, pulled her to me, though she still clutched Gene's vest with one hand. Her tears seeped through my shirt. "Goddamn him," she said.

"Come on," I whispered. "Sit over here." I ushered her to the sofa, then retrieved a box of tissues from a table on the other side of the room.

"You don't know how much you look like him," she said, smiling suddenly.

I sat on the sofa beside her and held her hand, her palm sweaty and warm.

"You know," she continued, "I'd like more than anything to be sweet about it all and remember only the good times, and let the dead rest in peace. But I can't do it. I just *can't*. I wish this would have happened some other way. Then I'd be able to think about it reasonably. If some drunk crashed into him or if he'd had a heart attack or something crazy like that, then this would be so much easier."

"I was just thinking the same thing," I said.

"But he did it to himself. Really he did it to all of us, you know."

"No, I don't think so."

She wiped her nose. "It's *true*. That's what Gene *did*. He left *messes* for other people to clean up." She started crying again. "What pisses me off is that he did this to get back at me, at you, at Angie, at everybody. He was trying to hurt all of us, hurt us in a way we would never forget."

I appreciated her bluntness, but I wanted, at this moment, to protest, especially with the body right there in the room with us. I'd known Gene his whole life, and could still see the baby, the boy, the goofy-looking teenager in the grown man, could see that boy even now in the corpse.

"I think you're wrong," I said.

"I'm not wrong," she said, "and we both know it. This was his way of getting back at the world, telling us all to fuck off, that we weren't there when he needed us, that we didn't take him seriously enough. This was a spite suicide."

She stared at me, waiting for a response. Her eyes were bloodshot, her lips quivered. I could feel my face flush with heat.

"Maybe we *didn't* care enough," she said. "We were all too selfish. But, shit, who isn't? You gotta live your own life."

We sat there in silence for a few minutes longer, and then I walked Gayle to her car in the back of the parking lot. The wind whipped hard, and her hair blew across her lips. She pulled the strands away.

"Thanks," she said. "I appreciate you staying with me. You shouldn't listen to me. I don't really know what I think or feel about all this." She kissed me on the cheek and then hugged me tightly. I put my arms around her as the rain started again. "We're getting wet," she said.

I opened her car door. She got in and then slid across the bench seat, her hand pulling mine along.

"Stay with me for a minute?"

I got in, and she wiped my face with a handkerchief from her purse. The rain pattered for awhile and then suddenly beat down hard, making swirling patterns on the windshield.

She rested her head against my chest. I draped my arm around her shoulder again, patted her arm. I could feel her heart beating against me. Or perhaps it was my heart. She lifted her head and tilted her face up to mine. I thought, okay, just this one thing, that's all, a kind of solace. But it was two moments, then three, and then before long our tongues were entwined, and our hands were on each other. It didn't seem real, and the unreality had something to do with the rain pelting down so hard, making the windows opaque.

"This isn't right," I said.

"None of it's right," she said.

The rain began to subside, and by the time we were done, it was quiet outside, the windows clear, revealing the lights from the parking lot. Inside, the car felt too hot, and I couldn't catch my breath. I thought I might suffocate. She started to weep. Her tears glistened in the dark.

"I'm sorry," I said.

"What do you have to be sorry about?"

I reached over to her, but she brushed my hand aside. "Go on," she said. "This never happened."

I opened the door and slid out, but then tried to turn and say something, to make some sense of what had just occurred. But she shut the door, started the engine without looking at me, and drove out of the parking lot.

The ground was soggy the next day, the day of the funeral. It threatened all morning to storm again. But then the sun came out, and birds chirped through the service. The preacher from Cheryl's church delivered the eulogy. He didn't know Gene, so he resorted to a call to faith rather than a personal memorial.

Rich refused to sit with the family. He stood on the fringe, fingering his mustache, scowling, shaking his head as though he was disgusted. When the preacher finished, Rich walked over to me and whispered in my ear, "Gene would puke if he heard that phony crock of shit."

He was right, but what did it really matter? The preacher was only doing his best on short notice. At least he didn't labor over the spiritual perils of suicide.

After the casket was lowered into the ground, people milled about, hugging and talking. I felt unexpectedly lighthearted. The whole family had not been together as a group in I didn't know how long. With Cheryl holding my hand, I moved among the relatives. I was thankful to have her by my side. She was a hostess and cashier for me eight years ago and counseled, cheered, and nursed me through the most difficult period of my life, after the freak accident that left me in the hospital for nearly four months, waiting for the skin grafts to heal. We married as soon as I was back on my feet.

Walking among the tombstones, the grass still soaked from the rain, the birds singing, I felt as if a burden had been momentarily lifted, as if the change in weather had helped transform this event into something tolerable.

But then, as I was talking with one of Gene's railroad buddies, I saw Rich and Gayle arguing near Gayle's car. Rich was jabbing his finger a few inches from her face, and she knocked his hand away, then turned and started to stalk off, but he grabbed her arm and pulled her back and yelled something, though I couldn't hear what it was. I waited for a moment, hesitant, not sure what I could say or do. Gayle and I had been avoiding each other. I feared looking her way, even though what happened the night before seemed long ago and forgivable because of the moment and our mutual exhaustion, confusion, and sadness. I started across the grass.

Rich began to say something else, then saw me approaching. We locked eyes for a couple of seconds, and something seemed to soften in him. I felt that perhaps my brother's anger might dissipate. But then he turned and ran to his truck, like a scared child, started his engine and roared off.

"Don't make excuses for him," Gayle said. Her face was blotchy with anger. She wiped her eyes with the back of her hand and opened her car door.

"What happened?" I asked, holding the door so she couldn't shut it.

"Get away."

"What did he say?"

"I shouldn't have come to begin with. I knew something like this would happen."

"What *happened*?" I asked again, touching her shoulder.

"Please, I'm asking that you just please please please leave me alone," she said. "I don't want to have any more to do with *any* of you. Please."

She moved my hand and shut the car door. In the backseat, I could see her boy, wide-eyed and wary, waiting for what would happen next. I wondered if he half-expected that I might do some damage. I was, after all, Gene's brother. Gayle started the engine, popped the clutch, and accelerated.

I walked slowly back to where Cheryl was standing.

"You better talk with him, Manny," she said. "You're the only one he'll listen to."

"Did you see the way he ran when he saw me coming?"

"He can't help it," she said. "He wants an answer like the rest of us, but there isn't one."

Suddenly, everybody seemed to be staring at me. I could feel my face burning. I started to speak, but stopped myself. I had nothing to offer them except my own shame and confusion.

When we arrived home that evening, Rich was sitting on our front steps, smoking a cigarette, the orange tip glowing.

"I'm beat," Cheryl said. "I'm going to bed." She kissed Rich on the forehead. "It'll be okay," she whispered to him. He didn't say anything, but I could see him soften toward Cheryl. She has this effect on people.

"I'll be up in a few minutes," I said, more for Rich's benefit than hers. I wasn't eager to stay out here with him any longer than I had to. I sat down on the porch swing and watched the smoke curling from my brother's lips.

"I hope I never see that bitch again," he said.

"You're too hard on her."

"You don't know her like I do. She drove him to it."

"You're not being fair. Gene was a pain in the ass to live with. He was a cheat, a liar, and he beat her."

Rich shook his head in disgust and flicked his cigarette in the wet grass. "Well, fucking hallelujah," he said. "Thank God he's in the ground!"

"I didn't mean it like that. But you don't know everything that went on between them. You don't know what their marriage was like. It's too simple to say she caused it all. And you can't let the dead off the hook that easily."

"Bullshit!" Rich stood, his body tensed. "The living get off the hook too easily." He paced the lawn. Blades of wet grass stuck to his boots. They looked like leeches.

"He admired you, Manny. He wanted to be just like you. And when he was in rehab last Thanksgiving, he kept talking about your accident. He told me that saving you from the fire was the most important thing he ever did in his life."

"He never talked to me about it."

Rich shrugged. "How could he? You didn't even go see him."

"I'd have just made it worse for him."

"That's bullshit, and you know it. You owed him that at least."

"Hey, if you want to blame this on me or Gayle or someone else, go ahead. But, remember, I didn't pull the trigger. *He* did. So what if he looked up to me? So what if he happened to be at the right place at the right time years ago and saved me. Yeah, I was lucky, and I owed him. But if the tables had been reversed, I would have done the same for him. Or for you. I'm grateful—I'll always be grateful—but does that mean I'm *responsible* for his actions?"

"Yeah, it does. We all are."

"Are you saying that if you go and jump off a cliff today, it's my fault?"

"You're my brother," he said.

"So what! That still doesn't mean I'm responsible. I couldn't save him. You couldn't save him. He was gone before we knew it. I wasn't the best brother. Neither were you. And the world's going to hell, and life's a bitch, and we're all to blame. Tell me something new. That story just won't hold up after a while. He died because he didn't want to live. Maybe he did it because he wanted us to feel like shit. It doesn't matter. It's the same outcome. And, ultimately, it was his decision. And if I wanted to do the same, there's nothing you or anybody else could do to convince me otherwise."

Rich shook his head and squinted his eyes as if he couldn't believe he'd heard right. "You really *are* a cold bastard, aren't you?"

I felt suddenly foolish. I had intended to be calm and reasonable, but now I was the one yelling, and I didn't even know if I really believed the words coming out of my mouth.

"I used to look up to you, too."

"I'm sorry," I said.

"Yeah, I guess I'm just another dumb son of a bitch."

He left then, and as I stood on the porch and watched him drive away, I felt like I'd buried two brothers on the same day.

Upstairs, I undressed and climbed into bed and pulled Cheryl close. "Are you awake?" I asked.

"Yeah," she said, but she wasn't. She'd had as little rest as I had over the past few days. I decided to let her sleep. What could I say to her anyway?

I closed my eyes, but my mind roared. I felt like I was trying to navigate between two cities on a child's map. The roads were erased or scratched out or never defined to begin with. Finally, just after midnight, I got out of bed and put on my work clothes. I hadn't been to the restaurant since Cheryl and Rich appeared, wet and shell-shocked, several days before, and I figured now was the time to go back and get some early-morning prep done before exhaustion really set in. Besides, the work with my hands would surely calm me down.

"Where are you going?" Cheryl asked as I was writing her a note.

"To the restaurant."

"Not today, Manny."

"I won't be gone long."

"Come here," she said. I knelt by the side of the bed, and she leaned over and kissed me. "Come back to bed with me," she said. "Warm me up."

"I'll be back soon."

"I love you," she said.

"I love you, too."

I kissed her, then put my head down on the pillow by hers so that our faces were together. She ran her fingers along my shoulder and through my hair. I rose, took off the clothes I'd just put on, and slipped between the covers. Her body was warm with sleep, and we made love slowly. Her fingers moved carefully over the scar tissue on my back. The night in the car with Gayle seemed a decade ago, and not quite real, but a betrayal nonetheless, though who I had betrayed wasn't clear. Myself, more than anyone else, it seemed. Afterward, I closed my eyes for a few minutes and dozed off, and then I startled awake. Cheryl pulled me close to her.

"Will you do me a favor?" she whispered.

"What?"

"Go see Rich."

I didn't say anything. She held onto me, continued running her fingers along my back.

"Please," she said. "He needs you to listen to him."

"I have listened to him," I said.

"No, you've talked *at* him, and you've *argued* with him."

I told her I'd be back before long.

"Soon," she said, and then closed her eyes.

The kitchen was not in the shambles I expected, but no one, except Saev and me, knew how to prepare the meat properly, and Saev was not nearly as fast as I was. There was plenty to do. I cut ribs and sausage, mixed tubs of potato salad, boiled red beans, wrapped potatoes in tinfoil, and sliced beef tips, rib-eyes, and sirloins. I fired up the pit and began preparing the ribs, flipping them every thirty minutes, basting them with the sweet, thick sauce. I'd been away from the restaurant for only a few days, but it felt like an eternity. It was good to be back, surrounded by the smells of food, the soothing swirls of kitchen heat. By four-thirty, I was halfway caught up. I dragged a chair in from the dining room and sat in the kitchen, sore and heavy and tingly-headed, warmed by the heat from the pit. I set one alarm clock to remind me when to turn the ribs again and another alarm to change the temperature on the oven. Normally, I needed no alarms. I could simply *feel* the time. The clocks were for Saev. But with as little sleep as I'd had, I didn't trust myself, didn't trust that internal clock of mine that I'd come to depend on. The rain began again, tapping out a staccato beat.

I closed my eyes and, half-dreaming, began thinking about the fire that nearly killed me. I was plunging into bankruptcy back then, partly because of the divorce, partly because of careless oil and real estate investments. I spent days driving around the Panhandle, from Charnelle to Borger to Lubbock to Amarillo, making promises and dignified and not-so-dignified pleas that sapped my energy and patience. I tried to do anything I could to stall, to finagle what money I could, but my trips to banks and creditors left me exhausted and empty-handed. Desperate, I'd gone to see Joannie, my ex, hoping she would help, let me take out a second mortgage on the house, which she'd gotten in our divorce settlement, along with half of everything else we owned. She couldn't, of course. Her lawyer wouldn't allow it. There, listening to her speak so rationally, calmly, I began to see how low I'd sunk, begging money from my ex-wife.

But instead of apologizing, as I knew I should, instead of leaving, I turned on her and spoke with a viciousness I rarely felt or exhibited during our marriage. I laid all the failures of my life at her feet. I let out everything that I'd prevented myself from even thinking before, even in the worst days of our marriage. She sat, stunned, watching me, her eyebrows stitched in disbelief. I felt my own rage expanding, along with the urge to completely crack open the ground beneath me, to strike out at her, to strike out at something, anything, to end this period of my life finally and dramatically. Then I heard soft crying. When I noticed our youngest daughter, Tammy, standing in the hallway, her eyes bugged, her seven-year-old body tensed as if to absorb a blow, I felt not only as if something monstrous had swallowed me up but as if I was the monster doing the swallowing.

I left Joannie's house at that moment, didn't say a word, just bolted for the door like a criminal. I drove around for a long while, and then went to the restaurant. A waiting line curled out the front door like a cat's tail. From the privacy of my office, I watched Cheryl, who I'd hired not long before and had taken out a few times. I was afraid I'd spoil whatever opportunity might be there for us. It all looked to be ruined. I'd lose the restaurant. Cheryl would find another job. To see her roaming so gracefully among the tables, smiling, talking easily with the customers, pained me. I would never have something that beautiful in my life again. That was how I thought of her at that moment—not just as a person, but as a beautiful *something*, a way of life that I would not have access to.

I felt caged in my office, overwhelmed by the need to fall apart, to break down in clumsy self-pity, but even that seemed forbidden to me here in my restaurant, busy as it was, full of people eating and chatting, my waitresses and cooks and busboys looking on. Just further humiliation.

So I drove to the Fina station. But once there, I felt seized again by my own anger and impending loss. Even the station would be gone soon. The bank had sent a foreclosure warning on it, too. I went inside the garage. *Where the hell was Gene?* Everyone seemed to be deserting me. There was a gas tank sitting next to the hydraulic fluid. The tank should have been moved. *Goddammit, why the hell hadn't he moved it?* I thought.

I wrestled with it myself, but it was too heavy, despite or perhaps because of my rage. I kicked at it, hard, and it wobbled. My toe stung. I fetched a dolly from the back and, cursing, eased the tank onto the little bed. I don't know what happened next. A spark. Where had it come from? From the dolly scraping the concrete floor? I'm not sure. I wondered later, as I lay in the hospital for months, if *I* was the spark, if my rage was capable of igniting the tank, like those people you hear about who spontaneously combust.

Then the explosion, the bright flash and enormous heat. The thick smell of gas and rubber burning . . . the tank, now scalding, on my leg . . . the dolly caught on my foot. I could smell my own flesh burning. I screamed, but my voice seemed far away. I should have tried to get up. I knew that. But, instead, I lay there, not far from the tire rack, transfixed, and watched as the tires shimmered in the heat. All feeling, all sound receded. Just sight and smell. I've never been a religious person, but there was something ceremonious and even seductive about the heavy smells. And comforting, too. An awareness that this was it, this is how my life would end. I no longer felt any pain. I gave in to the flames rolling out like banners, and then the windows of the garage broke soundlessly... and all for me. I began to crawl, but then stopped to watch the smoke rise, to watch it fill the garage and obscure the floor. I wanted the smoke to cushion me. I watched it as it moved toward me like a giant pillow. I didn't care anymore, and there was, I remember, a great sense of relief, even serenity, in the not caring. I closed my eyes.

The next thing I knew I was being lifted beneath my arms and dragged. I saw parts of my skin puddled on the floor, along with my burnt clothes. Then the sound came back. I remember the high wail of the sirens. Inside the ambulance, I looked up and there was Gene's tattered and charred coat and then his face, blackened and streaked with what seemed like ashy tears. He smiled and spoke softly, in a voice I hadn't heard since he and I were boys.

"It's gonna be all right, Manny," he said. "You're gonna be all right. Hang on now, just hang on."

The alarm in the kitchen buzzed, and I was groggy and hot. I rose heavily and opened the pit, felt the familiar waves of heat brush past my cheeks. I grabbed the long fork and absently turned the ribs, then slumped back down in the chair, disoriented and exhausted.

Why had Gene talked so much to Rich about this one moment in his life? By the time we reached the hospital, I was unconscious. When I came to, Gene had disappeared. Cheryl and Rich, Joannie, my kids, other family members came and went. But while Gene had saved me, pulled me from the flames, and nearly killed himself in the process, he was nowhere to be found. I heard he was in Houston, working offshore on an oil rig, but no one in the family knew for sure. I didn't see or hear from him again for another six months. By then I was out of the hospital, the crisis past, the memory of those moments in the garage, and the person I was during those moments, receding.

Of course, I owed him my life. What Gene had done was, by all accounts, foolish. He could have died himself. Even the firemen said he was crazy. And yet, I had always felt, on some level that I didn't even like to acknowledge to myself, resentful.

I resented that he'd pulled me from that fire and then disappeared. I didn't like feeling indebted to him. And surely he had seen that, lying there on the cement floor of the bay, I was still and strangely calm, waiting for the inevitable. I had, in fact, welcomed it. He was the only one who knew that.

I wondered what separated my accident from Gene's bullet in the heart. It seemed to me a matter of will and resignation. In the gas station, with my life falling apart around me, I had given up on my anger. I'd accepted my own death, and though I'd always been secretly ashamed of that fact, I could see now that it was that sense of peace that delivered me into this new life with Cheryl.

The other alarm buzzed, and I jumped up and clicked it off, changed the temperature on the basting oven, and went back to work. Cutting, slicing, mixing, trying not to think or feel so much.

Another hour passed quickly. At six-thirty, Saev arrived and was surprised to see me standing in the kitchen, my shirt stained with sweat and barbecue sauce, my face perspiring.

"What are you doing here, Mr. Manny?"

Saev always prefaced American names with a Mr. or Miss. The waitresses enjoyed it, teased him, called him a Southern gentleman. I liked Saev's cheerful formality, too. In Vietnam he had been an architect, but here he was simply a cook. Yet he had managed to bring his relatives to America by working for me. I paid him well, and he worked hard and long hours, double shifts, overtime to save that money. I've always felt proud to be a player in his family reunion.

"I couldn't sleep," I said. "I thought the place would be a wreck, but you stayed caught up fairly well."

"Not busy this week," he said.

"You did a good job anyway. I appreciate it."

"I am sorry about Mr. Gene. He is a good man."

"You think so?" I said, surprised by the insight, but also a little startled by the word *is*. Saev spoke English well, formally even, but he sometimes confused past and present tense, which in this instance mattered a great deal to me.

Saev looked at me as if this was a strange question. "Oh, yes. Good man. Tate brothers, very good men."

Saev hung up his jacket and put on his apron, pulled out two plastic tubs, got a box of cabbage from the walk-in and began cutting it for coleslaw. I poured myself a large cup of coffee, grabbed a couple of fresh rolls from the oven, and sat on a stool in the kitchen next to Saev and watched him work. I felt lightheaded from the lack of sleep and the heat. It was a strange feeling, though a good one, lucid but weightless. It reminded me of being in the hospital after the accident, the drugs blissfully untethering me from my pain, from my own skin, which had been burned so badly that many of the nerve endings were permanently damaged. The skin grafts were successful, but the scars are still, and will always be, bad.

"It must seem strange to you," I said, "that here in America people kill themselves when they actually have it pretty good. When they have no good reason."

"The heart always has reasons," Saev said, plunging the large stainless steel spoons into the coleslaw.

I left for home, where I hoped to hibernate the rest of the day, to fall into a dreamless sleep, but my mind was humming. I remembered that Cheryl had encouraged me to go see Rich. I thought it could wait, but then I started to feel uneasy, a churning in my stomach the closer to home I got.

The sky was black again with pregnant clouds, and I could smell the coming rain. I slowed, turned the truck around, and headed for Rich's trailer. The unpaved road to his place was muddy and potholed from the week of storms, and Rich's truck was splattered with fresh mud on the sides and grill. I knocked on the door, but no one answered. I went to his window and banged on it, but still nothing.

As I got out my keys, I saw wisps of smoke rising from the back of the trailer. I walked around, trying unsuccessfully to avoid the mud. Rich was slumped in a plastic lounge chair on the back porch, his hat covering his eyes, an almost-empty fifth of bourbon on a TV tray beside him. A green tarp was strung over the porch. A few feet away, inside a ring of rocks, a small fire burned. Smoke rose in an unsteady stream. He didn't seem surprised to see me there, as if he'd been expecting me.

"You want a drink?" he asked without moving.

I sat on the bottom step, just under the tarp. He handed me the bottle, and though I didn't really want a drink, not so early in the day and with so little sleep, I took a swig anyway. The bourbon burned, bitter and acidic, and I passed the bottle back to him.

"You been out here all night?" I asked.

"Couldn't sleep." He took a long swallow and then said, "It doesn't even seem real."

In silence, we finished off what was left of the bourbon, both of us looking at the fire and past it at the empty state land that abutted his property. Sprinkles of rain landed on the tarp, a few hitting my head and arm. Rich reached under his chair and pulled out another bottle.

"I'm sorry about last night," I said. "You were right."

"About what?" he asked suspiciously.

"I should have been there with him. I should have gone to see him."

Rich shook his head and smiled, cut the label with his pocket knife, opened the bottle, and took a drink before leaning his head back on the chair. "I saw it coming," he said.

"None of us could've—"

"No," he said, cutting me off. "I knew it was coming, but I just didn't want to believe it."

I wasn't sure I wanted to hear what he had to say. Rich leaned forward, stared at the dying fire. He spoke at first in a flat, cool voice, as if removed from the telling. I listened, reminding myself to keep my mouth shut.

"First time was a couple of months ago," he said. "He promised to fix my refrigerator, so I loaned him my key. He fixed it, gave me my key back. About a week later, I come home and his truck's out front, and my door is locked. I walk in and shout, 'Gene!' He comes running out of my bedroom, his face red, like I caught him jacking off. I go into the kitchen and start making a sandwich. He follows me, and without me even saying another word, he starts bawling like a goddamn baby. It was so weird. So I ask him if he needs some money because I know he's broke from alimony payments. But he just keeps on crying, not answering me. So I tell him to quit it, stop his goddamn blubbering in my house, go cry in his truck. I push him out the door. Literally. Can you believe it? Just threw him out. And he sat on my porch for another half-hour before he finally left. I ate my sandwich and watched TV the whole time."

"What was he doing in your room?" I asked.

"Looking for money, maybe. Nothing was missing, so who knows?"

"Why didn't you tell me?"

"Are you kidding? No way I was going to tell you or anybody else. After a while it just didn't seem like it happened, you know? We never mentioned it."

Rich took a drag from his cigarette, held it for a long time, then let it stream from his nostrils. He handed me the bottle again, and I took another pull and gave it back to him.

"Then about two weeks ago, Gene called me up in the middle of the night, and he said, 'Rich, I got a shotgun against my forehead.' Of course, that freaked me out, so I threw my clothes on and drove over, but he wouldn't let me in. I beat on the door, but he said, 'It ain't no use.' He said, 'I'm so damn tired. I just want everybody to leave me alone.' I said, 'Why in the hell did you call me then? I'm tired, too.' He said, 'I just wanted you to know.' I said, 'If you don't let me in, how the hell am I gonna help you?' We went on like that for fifteen minutes or so until I got pissed off and said, 'Go ahead then. Blow your fucking brains out.' "

Rich paused for a long minute, looked at the fire.

"What happened then?" I asked. I tried to keep my own voice even, calm.

"The next day, he came over, laughing, and said, like he didn't remember, 'Did I call you last night?' I told him, 'Yeah.' 'What'd I say?' When I repeated it, he just laughed. 'I was drunker than shit.' He wasn't drunk, and he and I both knew he was lying, but I didn't call him on it. Then he said, 'You ain't gonna tell anybody, are you?' I told him no, of course not."

Rich's chin started shaking, and he took a drink to steady himself. I didn't know what to do for him.

"He killed himself because I didn't want to embarrass him," he said.

"It's not your fault."

Rich stood up then and threw the bottle at the fire. The glass shattered on the rocks, and burning sticks flew in the air and landed on the grass outside the ring. The grass started to catch, but it was still wet, so the fire couldn't get any traction.

"It's not your fault," I said again, with more conviction.

The rain tapped out a rhythm on the green tarp over our heads. Rich looked like he was about to cry. His neck was tight, the veined cords showing through his skin. He shook his head a few times to control himself.

"I saw it coming," he said and started to laugh, but choked on it. "I knew it was going to happen, and that it wouldn't be long. I should've done something."

I rose and stood behind him. I could smell the liquor and the smoke from the fire and cigarettes. I couldn't remember the last time I was so close to my brother that I could smell him.

We waited there, neither of us saying a word, and then something strange happened. Everything seemed to shift into focus for me. I could see a squirrel shooting up a nearby tree. The smoke from the dying fire snaked thinly into the air, and I could see each tendril vividly. I could see each individual raindrop hitting the ground, the rocks, the porch. The shards of glass from the broken bottle glinted distinctly in the grass. I felt for a moment that I was on the verge of understanding something profound, that I would understand the meaning of Gene's death and what had happened these past few days, what purpose it would serve in our lives. I felt that if I just opened my mouth, I would be able to articulate to my brother and to myself what I felt. I started to speak, but then, just as quickly, the instant passed, like someone had dropped a curtain, and everything dulled a little as I struggled to recapture what I thought I realized. I'm not sure what it was now. I hesitate to call it a revelation, though it felt that profound to me. Whatever it was, it was gone, like the last wisp of a dream. I wasn't up to the moment, wasn't prepared to make sense of whatever it was I thought I understood.

Rich began sobbing. It was not loud, but his shoulders trembled, and he put his hands to his face. He was embarrassed, ashamed of his grief. I wanted to help him, but I didn't know what he needed. I don't think I've ever felt more helpless in my life.

I put my hands on his shoulders. "It's gonna be all right," I said and seemed to choke. I swallowed hard and then said, through the constriction in my throat, "We're gonna be all right." I didn't know if it was true or not. How could I? But it seemed important to say it.

The rain came down harder, pounding the metal roof and the tarp and the ground. We stayed there like that for what seemed an eternity, me holding onto my brother's shoulders, both of us staring out over the wet land as the sky darkened and the air chilled and smelled heavy and almost sweet.

Acknowledgments

I'd like to thank these editors for helping make these love songs better and for giving them good homes: Linda B. Swanson-Davies and Susan Burmeister-Brown, Sena Jeter Naslund, Hannah Tinti, Hilda Raz, Allen Gee, Sheila Sanderson and Melanie Bishop, Dinty W. Moore, Grace Dane Mazur, John McNally, Adriena Dame, Jarrid Deaton and Sheldon Lee Compton, Brian Bedard, and D. Seth Horton.

Thanks to Christopher Howell and the judges, editors, and staff at the Spokane Prize for Short Fiction, Willow Springs Editions, and the Inland Northwest Center for Writers at Eastern Washington University for honoring this book and for their hard work on its publication.

I'm grateful to my colleagues and students at Prescott College and Spalding University's MFA in Writing Program. The English Department at St. Lawrence University provided invaluable support and friendship during a year that I spent in Canton, New York as the Viebranz Visiting Professor of Creative Writing. I also want to thank The MacDowell Colony, The Corporation of Yaddo, and The Ucross Foundation (and Deb Ford) for residency fellowships, as well as the Sisk family for the use of their Durango home and Ronald Regina and Bart Broome for the use of their Palm Springs home.

I am indebted to my friend and agent, Jennifer Cayea, who has been both an excellent critic and my best advocate. Joe Schuster, a wonderful novelist and an ideal reader, has been my literary comrade, counselor, and one of my best friends for the last twenty-something years. And Wayne Regina and Tim Crews—my great friends, most valued colleagues, and writing retreat pals.

Finally, I'd like to thank my extended family, especially Brandy Cook, Lena Kellison, and Mike Thomason. And, of course, my children—Lena, Vivian, Tristan, and Carson—and my wife, Charissa Menefee, without whom none of this would exist or matter.

Willow Springs Editions staff contributions to this book: Aimee Cervenka, Olivia Croom, Christopher Cullen, Trevor Duston, Melissa Huggins, Ann Huston, Kristina Morgan, and Danielle Shutt.